AMELIA AND THE CAPTAIN

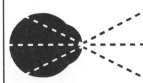

This Large Print Book carries the
Seal of Approval of N.A.V.H.

AMELIA AND THE CAPTAIN

LORI COPELAND

THORNDIKE PRESS
A part of Gale, Cengage Learning

GALE
CENGAGE Learning·

Farmington Hills, Mich • San Francisco • New York • Waterville, Maine
Meriden, Conn • Mason, Ohio • Chicago

GALE
CENGAGE Learning®

Copyright © 2017 by Lori Copeland.
Sisters of Mercy Flats #3.
Scripture quotations are taken from the King James Version of the Bible.
Thorndike Press, a part of Gale, Cengage Learning.

LIBRARY OF CONGRESS CATALOGING-IN-PUBLICATION DATA

Names: Copeland, Lori, author.
Title: Amelia and the captain / Lori Copeland.
Description: Large print edition. | Waterville, Maine : Thorndike Press, 2017. | Series: Thorndike press large print Christian fiction | Series: Sisters of Mercy Flats ; 3
Identifiers: LCCN 2016057592 | ISBN 9781410496997 (hardback) | ISBN 1410496996 (hardcover)
Subjects: LCSH: Large type books. | BISAC: FICTION / Christian / Romance. | GSAFD: Love stories. | Christian fiction.
Classification: LCC PS3553.O6336 A84 2017b | DDC 813/.54—dc23
LC record available at https://lccn.loc.gov/2016057592

Published in 2017 by arrangement with Harvest House Publishers

Printed in the United States of America
1 2 3 4 5 6 7 21 20 19 18 17

AMELIA AND THE CAPTAIN

ONE

Sister Amelia McDougal had turned out to be one colossal nuisance. And the last thing Captain Morgan Kane needed was a headache. A female headache. His patience was running thin. This newest delay, though small, had cost him valuable time, and for him time was running out. Why did he happen to be riding by when a jail wagon containing three nuns crossed his path? Even more puzzling, why would a band of youthful braves be terrorizing these particular women?

It seemed the good Lord didn't intend for him to reach Galveston by the end of the week. One delay after another. The horse had thrown a shoe outside Waco. He was forced to go clear to Waxahachie to find a blacksmith because the one in Waco had died. From there he'd run into a terrible storm near Henderson, where he'd been forced to stay the night in a flea-infested hotel. Sometime after midnight he'd joined his horse in the barn, trying to find a dry place to sleep. Early that morning he had ridden through Italy, a horsehair-scattered settlement, and stopped to help a woman carry a mattress out of her house. Seems her husband was ailing and the pad made him sneeze. The woman had fed Morgan a good dinner of fried catfish and corn bread to repay him for his trouble.

Now the recent Comanche threat had passed, and his thoughts shifted to the immediate problem — what to do with the sister he now had with him. Though the prospect was tempting, he couldn't leave her by the roadside, but it was clear that the young woman harbored a penchant for nature that would drive a sane man up a wall. In the brief time they'd been together, she admired or spoke about her fascination with low-flying birds, blooming flowers, rolling clouds, and glowing sunsets. It appeared that life in general enthralled this sheltered woman.

While Morgan could appreciate spontaneity, the sister's continual flights of fancy shattered his schedule and played havoc with his system of order. Lifting his face, he rolled his eyes when the sister appreciated a clump of weeds she mistook for flowers.

The horse had thrown another shoe and had almost gone lame before Morgan could find a blacksmith. The weather turned unseasonably warm and muggy, and his stomach was complaining loudly. He hadn't taken the risk of stopping for dinner, aware that the Comanche were young and exuberant and had their sights set on the woman.

If the interruptions continued, he would be in danger of missing his meeting with Elizabeth — but that was one appointment he planned to keep regardless of delays.

Sister Amelia McDougal viewed the last few hours as unsettling but far from alarming. If Abigail were here, she would say everything would be just fine. Stop being a worrywart. And she admitted she could worry with the best of them. At first she had been right put out when Comanche swooped down on the jail wagon, but when this nice Union officer rode to her aid and immediately restored calm, her confidence soared. Two additional riders had helped Abigail and Anne-Marie, so there was nothing to be upset about. The savages had been outwitted. Everything was fine now. And what a lovely early spring day! Sunshine, wildflowers scattered about the fields — it was a blessing to be alive.

Sighing, she admired the considerable

breadth of the Yankee's shoulders. The way he sat up tall and straight in his saddle. Very nice. He surely made an admirable sight. Undoubtedly he was taken or had at least a hundred women in love with him — that, or there was something terribly wrong with Texas women.

They had been together more than a day now, and she found him most cordial to her and capable. He was the most organized, masterful man she'd ever met, and she wasn't in a hurry to get home. He escaped those Comanche with hardly a sweat.

When this adventure was over, she was going to introduce him to her sisters, Abigail and Anne-Marie. Meeting such a fine, manly specimen might change her sisters' less-than-charitable feelings for the opposite sex. They would like this particular man. Though the officer was pensive throughout the ordeal, he had treated her with the utmost respect, seeing to her every need as if she were a welcome guest instead of yet another fly in the ointment.

Although they'd only met, Amelia had a hunch that this handsome Yankee took a fancy to her. The intuition hadn't been inspired by anything said or done, but she saw that glint of interest every time he focused those remarkable steel-gray eyes on her. Odd how two strangers seemed to gravitate toward each other. Although her knowledge of men would fit inside a thimble, she was positive this particular man found her interesting, though he would never confess his admiration. Men were intimidated by her nun's disguise, as well they should be. Yet she toyed with the thought of telling this man the truth, that the black cloth and veil were a masquerade — a very clever one, if not for the fact her conscience said it was a shameful camouflage.

"Oh, this is lovely," Amelia admitted when they made camp the second evening. It was uncanny how the man knew how to please a woman. How could he have known that she favored clearings beside wooded streams? Gurgling water, mossy stones.

Her escort quietly sidestepped her and then sidestepped her again as he went about making camp.

"Oh, here, let me do that," she scolded when she noticed he was doing all the work.

"No, if you'll just step aside —"

"I insist." Taking the branches from his arms, she smiled. "Now, you do whatever you need to do. I'll gather wood."

Sidestepping her a third time, he returned to his large auburn stallion to rummage through the saddlebags. "Hope you don't mind hardtack and jerky."

"You don't have bacon?" The only reason she and her sisters were in the mercantile yesterday was to help themselves to a few strips of bacon and some fruit. The store had an abundance of fruit and meat. Surely a few slices of bacon and three oranges would never be missed. And they wouldn't have if the clerk hadn't had eagle eyes and caught them in the process.

Kane's voice brought her back to the present. "No bacon. Hardtack and jerky."

"Eat without me," she said cheerily. "I only eat bacon."

Morgan Kane glanced up. "Bacon?"

"Well, mostly bacon. Sometimes, if I get hungry enough, I'll eat ham. But I love bacon." Humming beneath her breath, she scurried around the clearing, gathering small branches to feed the fire.

"Where is the nearest port?" When darkness fell, Amelia huddled closer to the fire's warmth. "Why is the fire so small?"

"Why do you ask so many questions?"

Her gaze roamed the campsite, and she was aware that she was chattering like a magpie. She'd always been chatty and never good at directions. She hadn't known east

12

from west the entire day. Before she knew it, another question slipped out. "Are we going anywhere in particular?" She had a right to inquire — her safety was in this man's hands.

"Nearest port is Galveston." He pitched the remainder of his coffee, focusing on the steam that rose from the ground. "I was on my way there when I encountered the jail wagon. We should be there by midmorning tomorrow."

She waited for him to ask the inevitable — why she was in the jail wagon — but apparently his impeccable manners prevented the inquiry.

Her eyes traced his tall stature. He was two heads taller than she. "What's in Galveston?"

"I have business there, but you will book passage home."

"I have no funds."

"I will be honored to pay for your passage."

"That is very kind of you." Her intuition was intact; he *did* find her attractive. Shame on him. For all he knew she *was* a nun. "What is your business?"

"I'm not at liberty to say."

"Oh." She fell silent. Then she gave an understanding nod. "Secretive business."

13

With the Civil War raging, most anyone was at risk of danger. She'd heard the mission sisters pray continually for the war to end and for brothers, fathers, and sons to go home. Peace would reign. Everyone was plumb worn out from the savagery.

"I'm sorry, Sister. I don't talk about missions." Stretching, he smothered a yawn. "I suggest we turn in. It's been a long day."

She nodded. "You said I can accompany you to the port?"

"It seems the only logical choice at this point. The war has brought all sort of riffraff to the streets. It's not safe for a woman to travel alone."

Tipping her head up to the sky, she sighed. "It's a perfectly heavenly night. I hate for it to end."

He huddled deeper into his frock coat. "I was thinking it's unseasonably cold for late March."

"Just look at those stars. Have you ever seen anything lovelier? The sight is worth a little discomfort." Winter was clearly drawing to an end, and spring couldn't be far behind, but tonight — tonight was perfect. Or was his company so stimulating that she hated for the evening and the rescue to end? She frowned, finding the fact that she hesitated to leave a man's company strange.

Very strange indeed. What would Abigail say if she knew that her sister was actually swooning over a *man*? She shook her head. Exhaustion fogged her brain. A good night's sleep would take care of her girlish fancies.

Silence stretched. She focused on the sky. Finally, "Captain?"

"Yes, Sister."

"My veil is caught on the hook of my collar. I can't lower my head."

He set his coffee cup aside and moved to help. Seconds later she was freed.

"Thank you." She flashed a grin and gazed up at him. "About your offer. It's very kind of you to pay my way to Mercy Flats, but I have no way to reimburse you —"

"Please, Sister." He lifted his hand in protest. "I would consider it an honor to provide your meals and safe return to Mercy Flats, but may I be so bold as to ask why you and your sisters were in a jail wagon?" His gaze focused on her black veil and white collar and the heavy cross hanging around her neck.

She felt heat rise to her cheeks. He'd dared to ask the inevitable, and the first prick of conscience hit her. He was so nice, and she was being so dishonest about her presence here. She had a niggling hunch that if she told this man the truth about her and her sisters' misconduct, he would walk away and leave her to the dangers he'd just said she faced. Best to stay silent about her private life. At least for now. Until they reached Galveston.

Focusing on the fire, she measured her response. Actually, she had little choice in the matter. She was penniless, and traveling alone would be poor judgment. She felt safe with this man, sheltered and protected. She couldn't have a more honorable escort, cool in the face of adversity, reserved, competent — but would he be so accommodating if she told him why she had been in that wagon?

"Why I was in the wagon is a rather long story, sir, and I realize you are weary from the long day." She changed the subject. "Are you from around here?"

"Washington."

"Oh, really?" She sat up straighter. "Have you ever met a president?"

"Washington Territory."

"Well, that's nice too. I've never been anywhere, but I'd like to travel someday — see the world. Is Washington far from here?" *You're babbling again, Amelia. Shush!*

"A fair distance."

Her gaze traced the width of his shoulders beneath the slightly rumpled double-breasted frock coat, and she heaved a mental sigh. The North surely must be bursting with pride to have a man like him on its side.

Over the years, she'd watched the Union troops going about their business and developed a certain admiration for the men. To be fair, the Confederacy had its share of notable specimens, but the handsome Northerners drew her. Their rugged spirit intrigued her, though she'd never breathed a word of her interest to anyone.

Abigail and Anne-Marie would say she was foolish for thinking any man worthy of second notice, but Amelia didn't agree. Men of every age whom she'd seen sitting straight and tall in the saddle weren't all that disagreeable.

Her eyes returned to Morgan Kane's tall form as he warmed his backside by the fire.

"My home is here in Texas."

"Yes, I believe you mentioned that. Mercy Flats."

"It's a tiny border town somewhere near here. I live in a convent — San Miguel — with the other nuns and my two sisters. I'm not sure how far away. Not as far as Washington Territory, I'm certain, but not close." She was never a good judge of direction or distance. "There's not a whole lot in Mercy

Flats except wind and dust." For once she felt she had his complete attention. "I was very young when I was brought to the convent — an infant. The only thing I remember about my parents was my mother's eyes. They were as gentle as a fawn's."

Her conscience pounded her. He was such an interesting companion. So nice, in fact, she suddenly felt compelled to be truthful with him. She knew he might find her admission startling, at best somewhat annoying, but she couldn't let him go on thinking she was actually a nun. The charade seemed almost sinful now that she thought about it. "Captain . . ."

His thoughts apparently returned to their earlier exchange. "No fruit? You only eat bacon?"

"Maybe an orange or a peach once in a while."

"Apples?"

"They hurt my stomach."

Moments stretched into even longer minutes as darkness settled like a mantle around them.

"Captain?"

Covering a yawn, he stood up to stretch his long torso. "Yes, Sister?"

"There's something I must confess."

From the turn of expression on his face,

she gathered that the prospect of listening to a long, dreary confession didn't catch his interest. The bedroll undoubtedly held more appeal.

"Can it wait until morning? I am unusually beat tonight."

"No." Her mind was firmly made up now. "It's important that I tell you now." If she waited until morning, she might have second thoughts. And the ruse, with him, was definitely deceitful.

"Very well. What is it?"

"Promise you won't get upset?" The last thing she wanted was to spook him — not here, where she couldn't make out a single thing in the shadows and she was completely at the mercy of his protection.

A slow grin — quite attractive, especially when she spotted the deep cleft in his chin — spread across his weary features. Her gaze shamelessly focused on the fascinating dimple in his left cheek.

"Let me guess. You spotted a great horned owl and neglected to mention it."

He was teasing now. Good sign, since he'd barely cracked a smile since they'd met. "No. I would have mentioned that immediately."

His playful grin fought with an ever-growing mystified expression. "I don't anger easily, Sister. I should think the past twelve hours have been mute testimony to my tolerance."

Getting slowly to her feet, Amelia lifted her hands to her head and peeled off the tight headdress and veil, freeing a mass of waist-length dark hair. Afraid to face him now, she quickly removed her collar and awaited his response. Would he walk away? Leave her here alone to fend for herself?

When the silence grew more palpable, she mentally braced herself for his reaction, fearing that she had misjudged his character. Was it possible that he would be so furious with her that he would order her to find her way back to Mercy Flats alone?

When the silence stretched, she wanted to cry. Oh, he was angry, and she didn't blame him. He had every right to be furious with her. He had unselfishly risked his life to rescue her because he'd believed that she was a woman of exemplary virtue. Now he could see that she wasn't righteous, that she'd only been pretending. Not that she wasn't basically honorable. She could be when she wanted to be, but she wasn't nun-righteous. Not a single law-abiding McDougal sister could be found in these parts.

"You're furious," she murmured when she couldn't bear the maddening silence a moment longer.

The captain stared at her, those beautiful eyes fastened like shiny spears to her heart. It was dark, but she imagined that if she could see clearly, she would detect a slow burn creeping up his neckline.

"Well, aren't you going to say anything?"

When he spoke, there was no sign of the earlier amusement. "Miss . . . or is it Mrs.?"

"Oh, Miss. Definitely Miss. I'm not married." That was the whole truth. She'd never met a man she would agree to spend her life with.

"Very little surprises me anymore, but this takes the cake. Why would a single young woman parade around the countryside in a nun's habit when she isn't a nun? That's blasphemous!"

She winced at the piercing tone.

"Do you care to explain your disguise?"

She drew a deep breath. "I'm a thief. The good Lord says it is better to give to the poor than keep everything to yourself."

His brows knit in a tight glower. "A what?"

"Not a *mean* thief," she clarified. "But nevertheless, a thief." She felt awful having to tell him, but in view of the circumstances, it seemed he should know the worst.

"A thief." He irritably shifted his stance.

"Yes. Crooked as a dog's hind leg. I

thought you should know."

"Thank you."

"You're welcome." A strained smile touched her lips. The admission hadn't been so hard. Actually, he had taken the news quite well.

"My sisters are impostors too — the ones who were in the jail wagon with me."

"Every one is a thief?"

"Not the good sisters who live at the convent. Just me, Abigail, and Anne-Marie."

"Who would be . . . ?

"My sisters. My blood kin." Goodness, the conversation had gotten so complicated.

"Of course. That's why the three of you were in the jail wagon. Because you're three sister-thieves dressed in nuns' clothing."

She nodded, smiling. "Exactly."

His bark stunned her. "I've squandered twelve hours and risked my mission for a bunch of thieving women?"

Smile fading, she backed up a step. "You said you wouldn't get mad." His face had become rather mottled. Yes, even in the dim campfire light, she could detect the subtle difference in shade. She feared she had strained the man's patience.

He strode around the fire and jerked open the straps on the saddlebags. After fishing inside, he produced a pair of wrinkled overalls and a plaid shirt and pitched the items to her.

"What is this?"

"Change your clothes."

"Why? It's a marvelous disguise —"

"Change your clothes!" His eyes skimmed her with distaste. "Sister. What is the world coming to? Women running around the countryside dressed as nuns, conning innocent people."

"Just men."

"Whatever! It's wrong."

The gloves were off. She heard it clearly in his tone. She stiffened, terrified to twitch an eye. "You are angry."

He nodded at the clothing. "Get out of that nun's habit."

"Do I offend your faith?"

"You do, madam."

"I honestly am sorry." She reached out to shake his hand. It was the least she could do in the awkward situation.

He stared at her extended fingers. Finally, with an impatient sigh, he took her offering and gave it a perfunctory shake. "Change your clothes."

"I'm sorry about the fib."

"Now!"

She jumped and backed toward the row of scrub behind her. He hadn't said he'd accept her apology, but he hadn't said he wouldn't. She ducked behind the bushes and unfastened the top hook on her gown. "I can still ride to Galveston with you tomorrow, can't I?" He wouldn't leave her here alone, no matter how angry he was with her.

"To Galveston," he returned, "and not a mile farther."

"I won't be a bother. You'll hardly know I'm around."

The grunt that followed did nothing to lessen her worry. Until now he'd been reserved and polite, but now that he knew the truth, would he be hostile toward her? Would she lose his protection?

Captain Morgan Kane didn't know her. Worse yet, it seemed he didn't want to know her. She'd seen the feeling of betrayal in his eyes, watched his attention turn to sheer disbelief. And no wonder. She would feel exactly the same if someone had tricked her.

When she stepped from the brush, he had changed into denims and a plaid shirt. With his military uniform draped over his arm, he brushed past her with a brief glance. The dashing Northern captain was gone. Watching his back as he spread his bedroll, she thought he looked like a poor dirt farmer, but when he rose to his full height and turned to face her, she recognized the pride in his military stance. He was still a captain, but not her former captain. The chill in his gaze exposed the degree of her deception.

She swallowed around the rising lump in her throat. His icy regard was difficult to witness, and she had no one but herself to blame.

He tossed a bedroll at her feet. "Turn in. We ride at daybreak." The curt response cut her deeply. A spark of resentment flickered to life. She'd only told him the truth. She could have fooled him forever with her nun's charade, but she'd trusted him with the truth, and this was the thanks she got for honesty?

Her chin lifted, and she brushed the bedroll aside. "You don't need to use that tone of voice with me. I understand instruction." She bent to unroll the pallet next to his. "I understand your disappointment, but I —"

"Go to sleep."

Her jaw dropped open. "I'll have you know, Captain Kane, that I —"

He rolled over and sat up so suddenly that she strangled a cry when his face came perilously close. His eyes bored into hers, and her breath froze in her throat.

"The rules have changed, Sister," he said

in a tight voice. "Go to sleep."

He was so close she could see the dark flecks in his eyes. "I truly am sorry for the charade," she whispered. She could feel the heat of his anger, yet she was undeniably drawn to him.

"Go. To. Sleep." Each word came out as if it were a fired pistol. "In the morning I will take you to the docks and pay for your passage to wherever you choose. Tonight I want you to lie down and keep quiet. Is that clear?"

Their gazes locked in a silent duel. She'd never been this close to a man, and the experience intrigued and terrorized her. She liked his scent — woodsy and manly but in a pleasant way. His hair lay in curly waves at the base of his neck. His forearms were a bit hairy, and the scant patch she saw above his shirt collar was dark. She had a hunch the captain had broken more than one fair lady's heart.

And she strongly sensed hers wouldn't be one of them.

Her voice cracked. "I understand that you're angry, and you have every right to be, but you could ask a little more nicely."

Without so much as a "Good night," he dismissed her and lay down.

Well, so much for men. If that was his attitude, so be it. Abigail had been right. Men — all men — were worthless.

TWO

Amelia stirred and opened her eyes. The beginnings of dawn lifted the fading darkness. She glanced at the bedroll, and her heart skipped a beat. The captain was gone.

Her gaze switched to the fire's dying embers. The coffeepot and even his saddle were missing. Her gaze darted to the tree where he'd tethered his horse the night before. Gone. Without a word, without a shred of evidence he'd ever been there except for the army blanket now snugly wrapped around her.

Maybe she imagined him. Perhaps her entire encounter with him had only been a dream.

No, he'd been real. Her creativity wasn't good enough to make up anything as remarkable as Captain Morgan Kane.

She sat up, holding her head in her hands. She'd never been alone, not completely. She would just sit here all day until she thought of what to do. She sat up straighter when she heard muffled hoofbeats.

"On your feet, Sister."

She lifted her head, and her heart leapt when she saw the captain sitting astride his horse, wearing a grim expression.

Harsh reality was back.

"Where have you been?" she snapped, forgetting for the moment that she'd missed him not a minute ago. "I was scared to death, thinking that you'd rode off without me."

"I've been shopping."

"Shopping!" If she weren't so grateful to see him, she would give him more than a piece of her mind. Her eyes followed his gesture to the scrawny mule standing behind his horse. "What's that?"

"Transportation."

"That thing?"

Turning his horse, he started to ride off. "You can walk if you like, Anabelle."

"The name is *Amelia*." She threw off the blanket and tried to focus. Apparently the man's hospitality went just so far. There would be no steaming hot coffee this morning. She walked to the waiting animal. "Where did you get this?" The mule was so skinny that his backbone stuck out beneath the woven cloth on his back. His coat was long and matted. Beneath his long lashes, he seemed to be regarding her mournfully.

Morgan rode back to give her a leg up. Before she could utter a word, she felt her backside land on the mule's sharp spine. She was about to voice a protest when she thought better of it. She wouldn't give the captain the satisfaction, nor did she want to risk the prospect of being left behind.

"New rules, Amelia."

Her eyes widened as his words from the night before echoed back to her. The rules had changed. Now he'd made up new ones? "All right. What do I have to do?"

"You will not, at any time, address me as Captain. The less you speak, the better." He raked her with bone-chilling regard. "I've been rethinking the situation, and you need to keep the nun disguise."

"I thought you said the disguise was blasphemous."

"Apparently the word holds no significance for you. Play the role of the good sister. That should keep us from suspicious eyes. The moment we reach Galveston, I will book your passage on the first vessel sailing near Mercy Flats. Understood?"

"Are you trying to hide something?" Abigail would say the man was up to something sneaky.

Without another word, he shifted the animals and led them out of camp.

A cold wind rolled in from the water as the odd couple rode into Galveston in the late morning. A watery sun glinted off the Gulf of Mexico as Morgan and Amelia directed their animals through town. Threading their way through the crowded streets, they both quietly appraised the situation. The town was oozing Confederate soldiers.

Glancing at the captain, Amelia swallowed. Was he aware that Galveston was a Confederate naval center? Even she knew that, and she hardly knew anything.

If Kane found the atmosphere threatening, he didn't show it. His features were fixed dispassionately as they rode through town.

Don't call him Captain. Amelia fixed her thoughts on Morgan's earlier warning. To address his rank would only set him off again, and he had been sullen from the moment she'd told him the truth about herself. A wave of loneliness washed over her. Were Abigail and Anne-Marie safe? Was it possible that she might never see them again? *O Father, please don't judge my sisters harshly. We have all sinned — perhaps me the worst.*

31

The dirt-poor farmer and the sister in a threadbare habit casually wove their way past rows of weather-beaten storefronts, blending in with the teeming crowd.

Mud-packed streets were filled with boisterous Confederate naval soldiers. Ship boys and officers alike, now roaring drunk, celebrated a few hours' reprieve from sea duty aboard steamy, heaving decks smelling of salt air and gunpowder.

Amelia's eyes anxiously scanned the area. Swallowing drily, she focused her eyes on the noisy mayhem. Bad things happened to other people, but never to the McDougal sisters. Sister Agnes once noted that everyone at the convent was blessed beyond measure, and Amelia believed her. People were always blessing the McDougal sisters up one side and down the other.

Amelia's eyes darted to the various signs tacked to storefront windows, offering a reward for the notorious "Dov Lanigan," a daring privateer who was barbarously good with a knife and sold women for profit. The evil privateer had quite a price on his head.

Spying a vacancy at a nearby hitching post, Morgan maneuvered the animals toward the railing and dismounted. Securing the reins, the couple stood for a moment, eyes fixed on the milling crowd.

Amelia edged closer to the captain and murmured from the corner of her mouth, "Better watch it. The enemy is everywhere."

He glanced down at her. "What?"

"They're all around us." She motioned with her eyes to their treacherous surroundings. "The enemy is everywhere."

Her voice carried like a feather in a hurricane.

She stepped closer, working her words through stiff lips. "Did you hear what I said?" If he was up to something sneaky, he had clearly led them into a nest of hornets now.

He gave her a glare that would blister the paint off a ship.

"What?" she asked, annoyed by his look. She couldn't do anything to please the man!

"Lower your voice."

"What?"

"Lower your voice!"

Color suffused her cheeks. Was he implying she talked too loud?

"Lower your voice," he demanded softly.

"I'm not talking loudly." She was appalled that he thought she was. Wasn't that just like a man? Try to look out for his safety, and all he could do was criticize. "I'm trying to warn you that you'd better be careful because this town is crawling —"

Her eyes widened as his hand clamped over her mouth.

She mumbled a garbled indignation. The dispute was starting to draw a crowd.

Well, that did it! He'd insulted her one too many times! Never in her entire life had anyone but her sisters ever told her to quiet down. Tears smarted in her eyes. He was the one putting them in danger. She got in his face. "Who are you to tell me to —"

"Quiet down," he whispered, his tone losing some of its sting. "Your voice carries. You're causing a spectacle."

"My voice carries?" She stiffened. "My voice *carries*!" And to think she'd once thought him to be a gentleman. A gentleman did not tell a woman her voice carried.

A passing couple turned to focus on the dispute. Shedding his hat, Morgan greeted the lady. "Morning, ma'am."

She nodded.

Grasping Amelia's arm, he ushered her onto the walk. "For your information, Captain Rude," she barked, as if they were alone in the desert instead of in the midst of the Confederate navy, "I was only trying to help."

Her voice bounced off the storefront wall. Turning his back to her, Morgan greeted another couple. When they passed, he said between gritted teeth, "I told you not to refer to me as Captain."

She glared at his back, unsettled by the lightning-quick turn of his personality. Where was the formal, courteous Yankee officer she had found so attractive? Gone, that's where. Gone just like her freedom. "I am aware of the danger."

She was unwilling to overlook his atrocious conduct. Some women might, but not her. She had misjudged him. He was an ill-tempered . . . snob. "Since I'm such a loudmouth, you'll want to be rid of me as quickly as possible."

Unbuckling the strap on his saddlebag, Morgan removed a roll of currency and peeled off three bills and handed them to her. "Two blocks down the street is the ship's office. Tell the clerk you want to buy passage on a vessel sailing near Mercy Flats on the morning tide."

"I'm perfectly capable of taking care of myself."

His dubious glance conveyed that he thought otherwise. "Just do as you're told."

She listened with crossed arms, tapping her foot impatiently as he went on to warn her not to talk to anyone, to keep to herself. He was treating her as if she were an infant.

"With any luck, you'll be enjoying a hot

35

meal aboard ship within the hour. Are you listening?"

She glared into space. "Yes."

"Lower your voice."

She whirled and marched off. She didn't have to take this. She didn't want his help. She would crawl to Mercy Flats on her hands and knees before she'd accept his money.

"Amelia!" All patience left his voice now.

"I can take care of myself, Cap— Mr. Rude! You don't bother your head about me one more minute."

"Amelia," Morgan repeated tightly. "Get back here."

"Go skip rocks."

In a few long strides, Morgan overtook her. Grasping her firmly by the arm, he halted her flight.

"Take your hand off my arm, or I'll scream."

"You won't. You've got more brains than that." His hand dropped away, his compliance assuring her that he was trying to keep this civil.

He smiled at the small crowd that had grown larger. Curious faces watched the vocal dispute taking place between the farmer and the nun.

"Just a minor disagreement," he assured

36

in a thinly strained voice, motioning for the puzzled spectators to move on.

A sturdy chap with robin's-egg-blue eyes stepped up, respectfully doffing his sailor's hat. "Is this man bothering you, Sister?"

Amelia refused to meet the eyes of her protector, aware she was causing a scene. "No, but thank you. My . . . escort's manners need a bit of work." She flashed an artful smile.

The crowd dispersed, and Amelia exhaled a disgusted sigh.

Morgan pressed the bills into her hand. "Now stay out of trouble." He turned and walked off.

Her eyes followed his tall form until he blended into the crowd. She'd show him. She didn't need him to get back to Mercy Flats. And he could bet his stuffy, spit-shined boots he'd seen the last of her. His earlier words raced through her mind. *"You'd better start eating something other than bacon — you're going to get scurvy!"*

She had no idea what scurvy was, but she wasn't going to get it. Not if he told her she would.

The afternoon was too nice to head to the shipping office. Not a vessel would sail until morning tide, so she had plenty of time to do what she wanted. She adored an adventure, and this certainly had the earmarks of a good one.

She wandered the crowded streets, peering into storefront windows, perusing the meager merchandise displays as if she had enough money to buy more than food and ship passage. She dawdled in front of the bakery window, staring at the crusty brown delicacies the baker was taking from the steaming oven. The big fat yeast rolls being set out to cool looked and smelled heavenly.

The captain had given her ample funds to purchase food, but common sense warned her not to squander it on cinnamon rolls. Her gaze fixed on a crusty loaf of bread, and she imagined butter dripping off its side. Streaming warm butter and jam. Raspberry jam, like the sisters made in big jars in summer. Her knees felt weak with hunger.

The captain's prior warnings about eating something other than bacon flashed through her mind. Her eyes traveled to the warm rolls. They looked so scrumptious. What if she purchased one and then discovered bacon two blocks away? She would have spent a portion of her money and be stuck with a roll that she might not have wanted as badly as she wanted the bacon that she might find two blocks away.

Why did life have to be so complicated? She wandered down the sidewalk.

It was downright chilly near the water. Her habit was scant protection from a stiff wind blowing off the Gulf. Abigail had told her March was usually mild in these parts.

Spotting a millinery, she crossed the street and hurried up the wooden steps. A bell over the door greeted her warmly.

She quickly stepped to the potbellied stove and warmed her stiff hands. As feeling gradually returned to her fingers, she began to browse the aisles, taking care to keep her answers to the clerk brief and to the point. She supposed a woman traveling alone should exercise caution even when dressed as a nun.

The clerk, a stout, vocal woman, appeared to have nothing better to do than visit. Amelia had frittered away the afternoon, and the store was empty now. She half listened as the woman went on about the weather and how her husband was down with his back again. Lumbago. Worse than usual this year. She had a long walk home once she closed up here, she complained. Amelia sympathized, though if she wanted, she could tell the woman about a real problem.

Hers.

The clerk leaned her elbow on the counter. "Did I mention my son-in-law, Jess? No good. Can't understand what my daughter saw in him, but nothing would do but she marry the weasel. Within two years she had two young'uns. Can you imagine trying to clothe and feed two babies with the war going on? Jess wanted to fight, but he couldn't. He gets heat exhaustion real easy and faints. Oh, he left one day and went to join the fighting, but after he fainted three, four times the commander sent him home. Told he wouldn't be a lick of help with that sort of condition. By then, Ella Sue — that's my daughter and Jess's wife — she'd grown accustomed to him being gone and rather liked the change. Don't suppose a wife should feel that way, but she did. Caused a fuss in their household for a while, but things finally settled down and they seem happy enough — leastways as happy as my Ella Sue can get. She was always a fretful baby."

The woman paused. "Anything particular you're looking for?" Clearly the woman wanted to close up and go home. Amelia would like nothing more than to oblige, but she didn't have anywhere to go. Fear suddenly gripped her. She was in Galveston, a strange town filled with rowdy men, and she didn't have a place to rest her head tonight. She would ask the clerk for help, but she feared she might send her to Ella Sue's house for the night, and it sounded to her like those folks had enough trouble without bedding down a complete stranger.

Glancing out the storefront window, Amelia noticed that it was dark now. Lanterns flickered on, and an occasional drunken laugh drifted from the sidewalks. Loneliness engulfed her. She had never experienced such a strong feeling of aloneness. She had nowhere to go until the ship left in the morning. She frowned. Oh dear. She had frittered away the past hours and still hadn't purchased ship's passage.

She hurriedly chose a warm, black woolen cloak and carried the garment to the counter. The captain hadn't said anything about buying clothing, but he should have. He'd prided himself on being so organized, but he hadn't considered her comfort. The habit was completely unsuitable for cooler weather.

"That be all for you?" the clerk asked.

"That's it." Amelia handed her a bill and waited as the woman counted out coins. Even with this impulsive purchase, she still had enough money for ship's fare. She'd just have to eat lightly.

"Can you tell me what time the ship's office closes?"

The clerk turned to glance at the clock hanging behind the register. "Closed about ten minutes ago."

Amelia gasped. "It's closed?"

"Closes on the dot. The man who runs the office even closes early if he's hungry enough. His missus is a fine cook." She handed Amelia her change. "Most everything around here closes early except the saloons. With all them sailors in town, they can carry on all night."

Well, at least she would be warm, should she be forced to sleep in the livery tonight because of her dawdling. She'd probably have to share her bed with the mule. She squared her shoulders resolutely. At least she'd have better company than she'd had the night before.

When she saw the clerk was about to wrap the purchase, she quickly waved the effort aside. "That won't be necessary. I'll be wearing the garment."

"Whatever you say, lovey."

Amelia removed her headdress, veil, and collar, and then settled the warm cloak around her shoulders. Handing the discarded articles to the clerk, she asked her to dispose of them. She wouldn't be needing the disguise any longer, and besides, the captain had made such a fuss about the disguise, she felt dirty wearing it.

With a puzzled frown, the lady disposed of the collar and veil and then ushered Amelia toward the door.

"You take care now," she called.

A blast of air nearly bowled Amelia off her feet as she heard the bolt slip firmly in place behind her.

Well, now what?

Lifting the hood of the cloak, she shielded her whipping hair from the stiff wind. She really should have bought ship's passage first thing, even though it would seem that she was letting Captain Kane tell her what to do.

The gnawing ache in the pit of her stomach reminded her that she hadn't eaten today. A hurried glance confirmed that the two eating establishments she had spotted earlier were dark and deserted now. She should have purchased a roll. One roll. The captain had given her sufficient money to buy three if she'd wanted. Anne-Marie accused her of being stingy, but no matter what her sister thought, she considered her ways to be sensible.

Drat, she hadn't been thinking again. Abigail and Anne-Marie often accused her of

not using her head, and she'd let it happen
again.

Stuffing her hands into the pockets of her
new cloak, she meandered down the sidewalk. She didn't know where she was going,
but she couldn't stand in front of the millinery and gawk. That would surely draw attention.

Street activity had slowed. The sailors
moved their horseplay into the warmth of
the saloons.

Her pulse quickened when she spotted a
tall, sinister-looking man step from the
shadows. Her footsteps slowed, and she
watched the menacing figure approach her.

Heart hammering now, she told herself
she should move on. Now. She should run!
She was alone and practically helpless. She
could fight, scratch, and scream, but a
strong man could overpower her. Her sense
of outrage stung when she thought of
Captain Kane. What sort of man would
leave a woman as scatterbrained as her to
defend her honor in this horrible port?

The form drew closer, and she released a
pent-up sigh when she saw that the shadow
wasn't as menacing as she'd first thought.
Actually, the man appeared almost friendly.
Clean-shaven, impeccably dressed in a
morning coat, a stiff collar with an im-

maculate cravat, and pin-striped trousers. Nothing threatening in his manner. When they met, he courteously stepped aside to allow her room to pass on the narrow plank walkway. With a congenial smile, he removed his beaver top hat and smiled. She hesitantly returned the greeting.

"A touch of chill in the air this evening," he observed.

"Yes, quite brisk." She stared straight ahead, afraid to meet his gaze. He might appear innocent enough, but he could be one of those friendly but depraved souls Anne-Marie had warned about.

"Take care," he said. "One as lovely as you should not be out after dark without an escort." He flashed a warm smile.

Her teeth worried her bottom lip. She knew better, but his was the first friendly face she'd seen all day except for the clerk's, and she needed a kind word right now. And truly depraved souls were never as polite as this gentleman.

Lowering his walking stick, the stranger changed his demeanor to one of a fatherly nature. "My dear, surely you are not alone in such a wicked town?"

Amelia instantly warmed to his kind eyes. He looked so benevolent, so trustworthy. Could she dare trust a complete stranger?

Abigail and Anne-Marie were adamant about such things. Never trust anyone, especially a man, they'd always said.

But Amelia felt so isolated, so uncertain. The area was dark and unfamiliar, and there wasn't a soul to tell her what to do.

"Yes. Through an unfortunate turn of events, I am alone." She glanced away, hoping he would see her distress and feel compelled to offer his help without her having to ask.

His left brow swept up to indicate his disbelief. "Forgive me if I'm out of place, but I sense that something is troubling you. Is something amiss?"

"Well, yes," she admitted. Something was definitely amiss. Morgan Kane had abandoned her in a strange town with barely more than a curt "Stay out of trouble" before he left her in this stew.

Sweeping off his hat, the gentleman bowed from the waist. "Théodore Austin Brown at your disposal. That's Théodore with an accent over the *e*. Permit me to be of assistance."

Concern was so apparent in his voice that Amelia didn't see how she could resist his generous offer. After all, he indicated he might be overstepping his bounds. What man would bother to say that if he had anything other than her welfare in mind?

"I don't want to frighten you, and I am quite certain you have been adequately warned about strangers, but you need help, little one. The wind is most sharp this evening. Please, allow me to buy you something warm to drink to ward off the chill."

Before Amelia could decide whether she should let him take such liberties, he had taken her arm and was steering her into a nearby hostelry.

"Well," she murmured. "I suppose it couldn't hurt." She would be in plain sight if this man turned out to be something of a scoundrel, though she couldn't imagine him being anything but genteel.

The hotel lobby was vacant as Mr. Brown ushered her behind a curtain into a small side room where four tables were set for dinner.

The waiter glanced up as though surprised by the unexpected arrivals. "Mr. Brown! How nice you could join us." He paused, his eyes focusing on Amelia. "Two for a late supper?"

Mr. Brown glanced at Amelia expectantly. "To begin, something warm to drink, if the young lady agrees."

Amelia's cheeks warmed, and she nodded acceptance. If she went much longer without eating, she would faint dead away.

Mr. Brown helped her out of the cloak and then held the red velour chair out for her. Closing her eyes, she sank into the plush softness, savoring the heavenly aromas coming from the kitchen. After he sat opposite her, the waiter opened a menu and presented it. Her eyes widened when she saw the prices. One meal would deplete her entire food allowance!

The stranger leaned forward and whispered, "Order whatever you wish. You're my guest, my dear."

"Oh, I couldn't." Twenty cents for a steak dinner! Highway robbery! And bacon wasn't even on the menu.

Placing his hand over hers, he smiled. "Then permit me to order for you." Lifting the menu, he perused the selections and then ordered two porterhouse dinners.

He returned the menu and turned back to Amelia. "Now, tell me. What is one so lovely doing on the streets of Galveston at this hour?"

While the waiter poured steaming cups of coffee, Amelia warmed to Théodore Austin Brown even though she much preferred bacon to steak. She couldn't afford to be picky tonight. Before she knew it, she was telling him the whole confusing story of how

she and her sisters had been rescued by three complete strangers from a band of marauding Comanche and were trying to return to the orphanage where they were raised. She omitted the part about the men thinking the sisters were nuns and about how they were in a jail wagon. That part wasn't relevant to the immediate story, and besides, it was embarrassing. What would this good man think if she told him she and her sisters had been running con games — however worthy the cause — across half of Texas for the past few years? He would be disillusioned by her, that's what. And she didn't want that, not again. Her candidness certainly had spoiled things with the last man she'd told about her past.

The stranger inclined his ear to her unfolding story, sipping from his cup and contributing an occasional sympathetic "Oh" and "My lands!" She and her sisters had indeed been lucky to escape unharmed, he concurred. Indeed, quite blessed.

"But I have been irresponsible," Amelia admitted, still smarting from the way Morgan Kane had dumped her like a sack of walnuts. Reaching for her cup, she took a sip of the hot liquid. The strong brew scalded her throat. Screwing her face into grimace, she reached for the cream pitcher

"I cannot imagine you being irresponsible," Mr. Brown said. "You seem very observant."

"Thank you. I was supposed to . . . well, actually, I was *instructed* to purchase ship's passage to Mercy Flats. But by the time I'd finished shopping, the office had closed."

"How unfortunate." Leaning back in his chair, Mr. Brown removed a pipe and small pouch from his right vest pocket.

"Now I don't know what to do." Amelia realized that she was being terribly straightforward with an outsider, but Théodore — with an accent over the *e* — Austin Brown, was the kindest and most sympathetic man she'd ever met. "Are you married, Mr. Brown?"

"No, I'm afraid I have never had the pleasure."

She was bad about ages, but she would guess him to be old. At least thirty or even older. The best years of his life had surely passed. "What a shame. You are a most astute man."

Mr. Brown filled the pipe bowl and absently brought the stem to his mouth. Apparently recalling his manners, he paused. "Would my smoking offend you?"

"Oh no." He was being so nice that if he wanted he could set his hair on fire, and she

50

wouldn't mention it.

The rich scent of cherry tobacco filtered pleasantly through the room as the man settled back on his chair, drawing deeply on the pipe stem. He dropped momentarily into deep thought as she sipped her coffee. The drink warmed her all the way to her toes. Coffee and an even warmer room made her sleepy. Admittedly, the thought of a warm bed and a good night's rest beckoned her.

Finally, Mr. Brown broke from his musing and bestowed another benevolent smile. "This must indeed be your lucky day. Quite by coincidence, I can be of assistance to you."

She sat up straighter. "You can?"

"Yes. Through a quirk of fate, an acquaintance of mine has a vessel anchored in the harbor as we speak."

"Really?" The good Lord was indeed looking after her. To be honest, she didn't know what she would have done if He hadn't sent Mr. Brown along at precisely the right moment. The good sisters said that almost nothing ever happened by accident, that God usually had His hand in the mix. Now she believed them.

"My friend is the captain of an older but highly seaworthy clipper."

"And your acquaintance is leaving in the morning? Sailing in the vicinity of Mercy Flats?" It seemed too good to be true. Skeptical, Amelia studied her new benefactor. "Is this true?"

"I would not mislead you, my dear. You have been through quite enough. My friend's original destination was New Orleans, but a storm blew his vessel off course, and he was forced to make port here in Galveston. I'm persuaded that when I explain your plight, he will gladly see you home. This Mercy Flats, is it far?"

She frowned. "I'm not certain. Maybe not too far." She had no idea how far home was, but surely Mr. Brown's captain friend would know. "Is your friend sailing in that direction?"

"I believe he'll be most obliged to in order to help such a lovely lady find her way home."

"Well . . ."

Leaning forward in his chair, Mr. Brown patted her hand consolingly. "I'm sure something suitable can be arranged." He glanced toward the waiter and motioned for cup refills.

Clasping both hands together, Amelia relented. She was simply too tired to object. "Oh, that's wonderful!" She frowned. "Of course, I'll purchase your friend's services."

"There's no need," Mr. Brown protested mildly. "I'd be most happy to see to your safe return —"

"I insist on paying my way," she contended. This man had been too kind. She fished inside her cloak pocket and pulled out the remaining money Morgan Kane had given her. She pressed the coins into Mr. Brown's hand. "If that isn't enough, I can get more when I reach Mercy Flats."

Mr. Brown refused the offer. "Nonsense. Passage will be small. Keep the money for the orphanage."

Keep the money for the orphanage. The man was an angel. God had graciously sent her an angel.

"Drink your coffee, dearest. Our meal should arrive soon."

Lifting her cup, Amelia relaxed, relieved to have the weighty matter settled. She had finally done something right. For a moment the situation looked as if she might be forced to return to Morgan Kane and plead for his help. She smiled. She didn't need him. She'd arranged for safe passage on the morning tide without his rude interference, thank you.

Over bites of succulent beef, Amelia chattered with Mr. Brown, who cut thick steak slices, clearly hanging on to every word she spoke. Not many men would be so openly curious or even care about her past. And it was rare indeed that she would eat beef. Not bad. Not bad at all.

"And you have no family other than your two sisters? You don't know the outcome of their recent misfortune?"

Amelia nodded, careful not to speak with a mouthful. "The San Miguel mission sisters are the only mothers we have known."

"I applaud such goodness and sacrifice, and I am confident that my friend, Captain Garrison, will be delighted to be of service. When we're finished here, I'll take you to his ship. You can settle in there for the night and be fresh for an early morning departure."

"This is so very kind of you." It was all Amelia could do not to nod off during the meal. The delicious food and sympathetic company . . . The day had been long and exhausting.

"My pleasure, dear." Lifting his water glass higher, Mr. Brown toasted her. "For such a rare beauty, indeed, it is my deepest pleasure."

THREE

Two figures sank deeper into the shadow between the buildings. Streetlamps burned low.

"I was beginning to think we'd missed connections."

"Sorry. I was unavoidably delayed."

The figures pressed closer together, conversing in hushed undertones. "Do you have the information?"

"Lanigan has been detained in New Orleans. Details are sketchy, but he won't be in port when expected."

The shorter figure swore, casting a wary glance to the entrance of the alleyway. "We have to sit it out? Wait?"

"There would be no point in going after him if we know he'll be coming here."

"This time he won't escape us."

"Not this time. He'll come to us."

"This means we'll be sitting here for days."

"Could be longer. My information is he

has been delayed. There was no timeline given."

A rowdy group of sailors crossed the alley, their boisterous laughter sending the figures deeper into the shadows. When the group had passed, a voice spoke again.

"We sit tight."

Silence. Then, "Do we have a choice?"

"None. I'll find you when the time is right."

"I'll be near. Let's hope this doesn't take weeks — or months."

The two figures parted at the entrance of the alley, walking in opposite directions.

A crescent moon had risen by the time Morgan entered the Drunken Monkey. He spent the entire day tracking the impulsive "nun." Yes, he vowed she was on her own and even meant it, but common sense wouldn't allow him to walk away from a helpless child. Amelia McDougal was far from a child, but she was incapable of dealing with a brutal world, so he'd spent the afternoon in the shadows, tracking her whereabouts.

She had done fine until she'd met a man shortly after dark. From what he could tell, the man was up to something. Thus his purpose in the hot, noisy Drunken Monkey when he preferred a bed and soft pillow. Amelia and the man hung together through dinner, and then the stranger walked her to a vessel moored in the harbor.

Why? Had she told him her absurd story? Had the man, like Morgan, taken pity on the helpless young woman? Or was there a sinister reason the stranger took to the young beauty under his protection? Women — both black and white — were being sold into slavery at an alarming rate. If he were to guess, he would say many of the large ships in port held these prisoners.

Morgan followed the stranger back to the hotel dining room and sat at a table in a dark corner, where he waited to order a hot buttered rum. Once he had given his order, his attention was drawn to the center of the room, where the stranger — Brown, someone called him — was now clustered in a small group of men around a large table. Loud but friendly males dominated the noisy pub. Morgan planned to stay long enough to determine whether Amelia followed his command and found safe passage to Mercy Flats. He doubted it.

His mind drifted briefly to the young woman he watched board a vessel in the harbor with Brown. Only his familiarity with Amelia's naïveté made him wonder if the vessel was bound for Houston or elsewhere.

She was an odd package. If he weren't so pressed for time, he might have been more accommodating and seen her safely home, but apparently she'd heeded his words and purchased passage, and she would be back at the convent soon. He was here only to confirm his guesswork.

A chair sailed past his table, shattering a long row of liquor bottles behind the counter. A fistfight had broken out, sending the occupants of the bar scattering. When order was restored, he returned to his chair, his attention centered on the group of men seated at the round table.

"I'm telling you, I've never seen anything like it!"

"Nay, guv'nor, you're puttin' us on," another scoffed.

"I swear on my mother's grave, it happened exactly as I said." Brown threw back his head and laughed uproariously. "The silly little twit offered to pay me!" The pub vibrated with male merriment.

"You actually mean she wanted to *pay* you to book her passage on the *Black Widow*?" another hooted. "And I suppose you took the offer!"

"Of course not. I am a gentleman. I offered to pay her way."

Another round of hoots broke out.

"This woman must be ugly as sin," a man sitting to Brown's right surmised in a droll tone.

"On the contrary." Brown's smile faded. "She's a comely young beauty lying at this very moment in her bunk aboard the *Black Widow.* She's really quite lovely and will bring a pretty price on the market."

The men rocked back in their chairs, clutching their sides.

Silly twit. Rare beauty. Morgan mentally groaned. Amelia McDougal was seriously testing his stamina. His drink arrived, momentarily distracting him.

"It's a stroke of luck, to be sure," the well-dressed man mused as laughter subsided. "I usually have to knock them senseless, tie them up, and drag them to the ship. But this one just up and insisted that she pay for the privilege. Wouldn't have it any other way." With a snort, he burst into laughter again.

"Is she securely snared?"

"Ah yes. The lovely nightingale is safely in her nest, and I can assure you, gentlemen, that she, fairest of the fair, will bring top price from Lanigan."

"Heard this Lanigan likes them young and impressionable as new-fallen snow," a man observed.

"That he does." Brown leaned back to light a pipe. "And that she is. Miss McDougal will bring a handsome price."

"You know Lanigan personally?"

"Never met the man, but I've heard of his preferences. Only wise to know the market one's selling to, wouldn't you say, gents?"

The men nodded in agreement.

"This Lanigan — is he as good as his reputation?"

"None better," Brown confirmed. "He is the king of the seas and master of treachery." He winked. "It is a pleasure to work for him."

"Not the Sunday school type, eh?"

The remark brought another round of raucous laughter.

Talk continued about Dov Lanigan's expertise with a knife and a woman. The heartless privateer with an exorbitant price on his head was rumored to be unrivaled in his field.

"How do we know we can trust him?" said another. "None of us has ever met him. How can we be sure he won't cheat us?"

Exhaling smoke from his pipe, Brown smiled. "I'll take care of Lanigan. His reputation doesn't intimidate me. He's a man, same as us, making a living best as he can. You don't run blockades and sell contraband for as many years as I have without risking your neck and sullying your reputation. But those days are over, gentlemen. Dealing in stolen women is a lot easier and a lot less risky. Hauling their whining carcasses across the sea is a bothersome task but not without rewards, my friends." His smile grew sly. "Not without a few rewards."

Morgan tossed the last of his drink down. The image of Dov Lanigan surfaced in his mind. The picture portrayed a dark-haired man, tall, about Morgan's age, without distinguishing features or scars. A man could walk past the notorious scum on the streets and never know he was wanted for high treason.

"I'm for selling the woman here," one of the men challenged. "If this one is as beautiful as you say, she'll bring top price right here in Galveston. Why split the bounty with Lanigan?"

"No!" Brown snapped. "Once Lanigan sees Amelia McDougal, he'll want her for his own. Nary a man who sees her could resist the temptation, and if the boss wants her, he'll pay even more for her." A sly grin crossed the man's features. "He'll not like it, but he knows money speaks."

"I say a bird in the hand is worth two in

the bush," another interjected. "I say we sell her right here, right now, tonight!"

The other men added their impassioned, rowdy agreements.

"Gentlemen, gentlemen, keep your heads. From what I've seen of our other women, they'll bring a mere pittance compared to what this woman will, if what Brown says is true," another argued.

Morgan shifted in his chair. How, in the brief time since he had left her, had she managed to fall into the clutches of these unscrupulous thugs?

"I'm still running things, and we do as I say!" Brown snapped. "A deal is a deal. Lanigan's brother has assured me Lanigan will pay top price for any woman I bring him of exceptional beauty. Now, gentlemen, you would not have me go back on my word? There is, after all, honor to consider, even among thieves."

"I'm relieved to hear it. I was starting to wonder," a deep voice rumbled from the darkest corner of the pub.

Swiveling in their seats, the men scanned the shadows.

"Who's there? Show yourself," Brown commanded.

Morgan calmly slid his hand inside his boot, touching the butt of his dagger. He was playing with fire now, but he couldn't allow the McDougal woman to be sold into bondage — though the thought was mildly tempting.

A burly man, eyes narrowed, went for his pistol. "I know how to rid us of nosy rats!"

Coming to his feet, Morgan set the dagger on its course. In the wink of an eye, the knife pinned the sleeve of the man's shirt solidly to the post. The man's pistol discharged harmlessly into the air before clattering to the floor.

Pushing back from his table, Brown rose to face the marksman. "There is only one this good with a knife. Dov Lanigan — I thought you were delayed."

Emerging from the shadows, Morgan casually strolled over to retrieve his knife. Brown had said he'd never met Dov Lanigan. Morgan was going to have to trust his word. The owner of the pistol mumbled and rubbed his shoulder as he turned away from Morgan's cold, measuring eyes.

"Dov Lanigan?" Brown repeated softly. "The manner in which you are dressed, like an impoverished farmer, I never suspected."

Morgan fixed him with a cold stare. "If I were you, Mr. Brown, I'd be more careful about my public conversations."

Brown repented. "I'm sorry, Mr. Lanigan,

I wasn't thinking." Fumbling for a chair, he offered a seat to the living legend. "It is a pleasure to finally make your acquaintance." He extended his hand. "Odd that we've been doing business for . . . what? A year? And I haven't had the pleasure."

The two men shook. Apparently Lanigan sent his runners to purchase the women.

When Morgan was seated, Brown nervously signaled the bartender for a round of drinks.

"You took me by surprise," Brown admitted as he pulled his chair up to the table. "I understood you were delayed in New Orleans."

"I was, but unexpected business made it necessary that I be here tonight." Amelia's safety should no longer be his concern, yet he could hardly stand by and knowingly let her be sold by this unscrupulous warthog. And if Dov Lanigan was nearby, all the better. Morgan would be back on track with his mission, and the costly delays would prove to be blessings. The Lord did work in mysterious ways.

The drinks arrived. Morgan methodically drained his glass, stalling for time. Now what? He was committed to be Lanigan, but he wouldn't be able to carry on the ruse indefinitely. Brown would catch on to the ploy, and both Morgan's and Amelia's lives would be at risk.

Some of the men wiped their hands across their lips when they finished.

"Where's the woman?" Morgan asked.

"Safely aboard the *Black Widow*," Brown assured him.

"She's uncommonly beautiful, you say?"

"Ah, uncommonly so. Eyes the color of spring grass, rich carmine hair, and a figure men would surely go to their graves for. She'll bring twice what you pay for her."

"An amount which I assume will be considerable?"

Brown's smile grew sheepish. "You pay for quality — isn't that what they say?"

"I'm curious about one thing. If she's so lovely, why not keep her for your pleasure?"

Brown chuckled. "I see that you are not a fool. There isn't anything I own that isn't for sale at the right price. She is yours if you want her. It's your good fortune that one so exceptionally lovely should happen into my hands. That isn't often the case."

Morgan couldn't stall any longer. The ruse could be over as quickly as it had started. With a cool smile, he said quietly, "Take me to this most lovely one."

"Certainly." Shoving back from the table, Brown stood up. "If you'll follow me."

Morgan nodded to the others. "You will excuse us, gentlemen?"

A moment later the two men left the bar to view the spoils of the trade.

FOUR

Something fishy was going on. And the smell wasn't just the revolting stench permeating the old clipper. Amelia couldn't say what, but something was terribly wrong. She'd felt it the moment Mr. Brown brought her aboard. Her gaze roamed the tiny cabin smelling of dead fish. What had she gotten herself into this time? The image of Morgan Kane flashed through her mind, and she groaned, glad that Morgan couldn't see her now. Mr. Brown was nice, but his friend's ship was deplorable. No wonder the captain of this vessel had so little to do that he could drop everything and see her back to Mercy Flats. The ship was a disgrace to the ocean.

Rolling off the narrow bunk, she tiptoed to the door, listening. When she'd come aboard, she noted how the old vessel creaked under the weight of the heavy timber as it rocked back and forth in the water. The ship was large, with heavy masts and yards. The old boat wasn't pretty, but she imagined it served a purpose. Exactly what, she wasn't sure.

Straining closer to the door, she listened more intently. She was certain she'd heard a woman sobbing.

She returned to the bunk and sat down to think. Her gaze roamed the tiny quarters. She didn't know anything about ships, but common sense told her Mr. Brown had overpaid to travel on this one. The quarters were plain and cramped. And reeking of dead sea life. Even Mr. Brown's captain friend smelled as if he hadn't seen soap and water in months.

She sat upright when the sound came to her again. A low, despairing wail amid creaking timbers.

Slipping from the bunk, she opened the door a crack and peeked at the narrow, deserted passageway. A whale oil lantern on the wall burned low, barely illuminating the narrow corridor.

Straining to hear, she listened as the sound grew more distinct.

Glancing behind her, she spotted a candle sitting on the washstand. She reached over and grasped it, allowing the door to swing wider.

Moving cautiously into the hallway, she

paused to listen. Her surroundings made her uneasy. Something felt evil about the old craft, an impression she was powerless to explain. She wished she had waited until morning and then bought a ticket to Mercy Flats on the stagecoach, even if she'd been forced to wait a few days. It might have taken her longer to get home, but the money would have been better spent.

Feeling her way down the corridor, she followed the sound of weeping. The oil lamp provided barely adequate light, casting elongated shadows through the passageway.

When she neared the end of the hallway, she noticed a door slightly ajar. She could barely make out the silhouette of a young girl sitting alone on a narrow cot, sobbing. A rush of pity flooded her. The poor girl was probably traveling alone and as frightened as she was.

She moved closer, tapping softly on the door. "Hello?"

When she received no invitation to enter, she peeked around the door into the cramped quarters that were larger but just as unpleasant as her own. The ship's captain should be ashamed to operate such a disorderly establishment. The good sisters said cleanliness was next to godliness, but it didn't appear either applied here. She didn't see how the ship's owners could hope to maintain a thriving business when they apparently cared so little for their customers' comfort.

"Hello." Amelia summoned a pleasant smile for the girl, who appeared to be very young. Perhaps barely into her teens.

The girl's head shot up, and Amelia saw that she was not only crying but was pale and appeared disoriented.

"Don't be afraid," Amelia began. "I heard you crying, and I wondered if there was anything I could do." Her words faltered when she noticed the young girl wasn't alone. Squatting along the walls of the cramped room were other young women of varying ages, all looking at her with equally desperate expressions. Mentally counting, Amelia decided there were nine in this cramped rat hole.

For a moment no one spoke. Finally, the girl on the cot choked out in a raspy whisper, "What do you want?"

"I heard you crying. Is there something I can do to help?"

"Help?" The girl looked at her as if she had suddenly grown horns.

"Yes — you were sobbing. The accommodations are wretched, aren't they?" If Amelia had it to do over, she would just tell

Mr. Brown thank you but no thank you for his offer of assistance. The accommodations were disgraceful, and she'd venture that the food would be even worse.

A slender young girl in the far corner spoke up. "Who are you?"

"A passenger. I, too, find the ship deplorable," Amelia confided, wondering why the women had congregated in such tiny quarters. She felt the lines in her forehead narrow when she noted the bindings on the girls' wrists.

"A passenger?" a dark-haired older woman in the opposite corner mocked.

Amelia smiled. "I came aboard about an hour ago." She glanced around the narrow quarters, suspicion starting to nag her. "Why are your hands bound? And why are you all in the same room? Are you traveling together?"

Companionship with other women her own age could be just the thing she needed to boost her sagging spirits during her return to Mercy Flats. But the bound hands . . . Reality slowly dawned on her, and she gasped.

A young woman with incredibly unkempt blonde hair struggled to her feet. "Really now. You're a 'passenger'?"

Amelia's heart hammered in her throat.

"Why are your hands bound?" She dreaded the answer. Her life had not exactly been a cup of tea lately. But bound hands? Tears? She shook her head, willing the truth to go away. Hadn't she suffered enough? *Please don't let this be the obvious,* she silently prayed.

"We're playing a game," the dark-haired woman returned in a listless tone. "Please, join us."

"Elizabeth," one warned. "Don't take your frustrations out on her. Can't you see she isn't aware of what's happening?"

"We're on our way to hell," the one called Elizabeth said. "She might as well know it."

To hell? Amelia recoiled. Well, that was ludicrous. Mr. Brown had purchased a ticket to Mercy Flats!

"Is there a Hell, Texas?" Amelia asked, still not comprehending the situation. There very well could be. She hadn't traveled very far from Mercy Flats.

The hard-edged woman rose from her bunk. "Try again, lovey."

Realization slowly dawned on Amelia. "You don't mean hell, as in a blazing inferno?"

"You got it."

Amelia sank to the soiled mattress, the woman's words ringing in her ears. Lifting her eyes, Amelia confronted her. "You're not making a lick of sense."

"Maybe she really doesn't know, Elizabeth," a dirty, blonde-haired girl said softly.

"Not know? Does she think she's on an ocean voyage? On this tub?"

Amelia nodded. "Yes, a short one to Mercy Flats."

Elizabeth turned away, contempt shining in her eyes.

A thin girl stood unsteadily and came over to kneel beside Amelia. "You really don't know what's going on, do you?"

Amelia was grateful for the kindness she saw in the girl's large oval eyes. The others seemed so cold and hostile. "I'm confused," she admitted.

"You're more than confused," Elizabeth said. "You're a prisoner, dearie."

Amelia bolted to her feet. She bit her lip to keep from bursting into tears. This couldn't be! "A prisoner! There are no bolts or bars on the doors! What are you talking about?"

"It's true," others whispered. A brunette spoke. "There may be no bars on the doors, but we are watched day and night. If we were to try to escape, we would be shot on sight."

"Prisoners?" Their words made no sense.

Nothing had made any sense for hours now!

The girl on the bunk nodded. "We're prisoners."

"Of whom?" Amelia demanded to know.

"Prisoners of an evil man by the name of Austin Brown," another supplied.

"Théodore Austin Brown?" Amelia asked.

"I see you've met him," Elizabeth said.

There was something about Elizabeth that Amelia resented. She'd sensed it the moment she'd stepped into the room. She didn't know what it was, but it was there as plain as day. Perhaps it was the coldness in her eyes or the razor-sharp edge to her voice. One thing was certain — they would never be friends.

"What would Mr. Brown want with me?" Amelia asked. "I only met him hours ago."

Elizabeth gave a harsh snort. "Undoubtedly he knows you."

"He befriended me."

"He hoodwinked you. The same as he did all of us."

"I don't believe it!"

"Believe it."

This was terrible. Ghastly! Amelia's gaze roamed the cramped quarters. The women were stuffed in here like sausage. Had she jumped from the frying pan into the fire? "What does Brown plan to do with us?"

The girls exchanged hesitant looks, but Elizabeth seemed to take delight in telling her. "He plans to sell us."

"Sell us? Into slavery?" Amelia reached for support. This was even worse than she imagined. Abigail had once told her about the scurrilous practice among thieves, and now Amelia was living the bad dream! Could life get any worse?

"Do I have to draw you a picture?" Elizabeth's words hung heavily in the air.

"Sold — to do what those painted ladies do that work in saloons?" Amelia whispered. She'd heard of such wicked things, but such revulsion was for worldly, tainted women, not her — or these innocent-looking girls.

The girl on the cot broke into sobs. "It's so awful. I'd rather die than be sold for a man's pleasure. To be a soiled dove!"

Another started weeping, and before long, they were all sniveling. All except Elizabeth. She stared at Amelia, whose ears burned with shame. She felt dirty just listening to the exchange.

"Now listen to me," she said. "I don't know what's going on, but I know one thing. I do not intend to be sold. And the moment Captain Kane gets word of this atrocity — and he will, because he seems to know everything — he'll rescue us." Now that shock was wearing off, she could think clearly. Soiled dove indeed! Over her dead body!

Leaning back on a bunk, Elizabeth casually rolled a cigarette. "Captain Kane?"

"Yes — a man who will not let this atrocity go unnoticed." Amelia watched with fascination when she struck a match with her thumbnail, lit the cigarette, and began to blow lazy smoke rings at the ceiling.

The young woman sent Amelia a snide glance. "You know Captain Morgan Kane? How can that be?"

"I just do — do you know him?" She looked the sort that Morgan would fall for. Pretty, in a wild way.

"Then pray tell, dear. Tell us what you and Morgan Kane plan to do so we can all 'refuse' to go along with Théodore — with the accent over the first *e* — Austin Brown's plans." She blew a series of little round O's toward the ceiling.

"Well, I'm not sure what I'll do, but I'll do something. Captain Kane will do something." *Captain Kane thinks you're safely out of his hair! He couldn't possibly know what you've done this time.*

Elizabeth appeared to doubt her claim. "Where is this Kane, this knight in shining armor? We could certainly use the man about now."

"He's around, I can assure you." Morgan had indicated he wouldn't be leaving until morning. She must get a message to him quickly. But how? If the others were right, she was also a prisoner. Oh, she should have known not to trust that deceiver Austin Brown! He tricked her! He wined and dined her and then sold her like a load of cabbage.

Elizabeth casually extended the cigarette to her. "Smoke?"

Amelia shook her head. Elizabeth was the first woman she'd ever met who smoked. The sisters would smack this young lady's hands and wash the tobacco out of her mouth with lye soap.

The youngest of the girls slipped to Amelia's side. "Can you really save us?" Her eyes focused on Amelia with open trust.

"Do you know where they're taking us?"

"I overheard one of the men say something about New Orleans," one ventured.

"New Orleans?" Amelia's heart sank. A decadent city to be sure. Abigail had told her about the red-light district there and of the music houses where women danced as they took off their clothes before men. Abigail read more books than she did. Many more. Until now, Amelia was sure such rumors about the French Quarter were wildly exaggerated. Perhaps not, she conceded. Discovering that she was aboard a ship of women bound for the worst kind of slavery suddenly made all other evils more plausible.

"We'll have to escape," Amelia said. "Since they haven't locked us in our rooms, we can manage it. They can't watch all of us every hour of the day and night."

Elizabeth boldly sent another series of smoke rings spiraling toward the ceiling. "Are you willing to wager your life on it?"

"She's right," another said. "There are dozens of men aboard ship, and they're watching us like hawks." The speaker's eyes focused on a dark-skinned girl. "Ask her. She tried to escape, and they caught her. Ask her what they did."

The girl turned away, biting her lower lip.

The horror of their predicament slowly seeped into Amelia's consciousness. "How long have you been here?"

The women gave varying accounts of their captivity, ranging from hours to weeks. Some had been captured far away and some as near as Galveston.

Elizabeth's eyes narrowed as she met Amelia's eyes with a mixture of contempt and resignation. "If the storm hadn't blown this clipper off course, the women would be in New Orleans by now. And I wouldn't be aboard. I've been here two hours, and I have no trouble understanding my predicament. So tell us, Miss Innocent, how do you intend to inform your friend Kane about our circumstances?"

Amelia glanced away when she felt tears swell. She hadn't the slightest hint of Morgan's whereabouts. The severity of her situation rose quickly to mind, and with it came a knot of desperation. Despair filled her. It was entirely possible that she would never see home, Abigail, or Anne-Marie again.

The thought was like a dagger plunged to her heart.

Oh, Morgan, where are you? I'm sorry I've caused so much trouble. The noble captain would never find her here.

Her blessings had suddenly come to an abrupt halt.

Wind gently rocked the old clipper back and forth as the half-moon dipped lower in the sky. Two men approached the gangplank, their shoulders hunched against the damp gusts.

A shout rang out. "Who goes there?"

"Permission to board," a voice called back. "That you, Brown?"

"It's me."

"Come aboard, mate!"

The two men quickly crossed the gangplank and stepped aboard the ship.

Brown addressed a burly Welsh packet rat as they stepped aboard. "The captain in his quarters?"

"He is, but don't disturb him." Packet rats were a breed of their own. They were wild, rough men, commonly of English, Irish, or Welsh origin, who understood no law but force. Dirty, uncouth, ignorant bullies, they nonetheless were superb sailors and feared neither man nor weather.

"He'll see me," Brown said.

The smell of Stockholm tar coming from the rigging hung heavily in the air when Morgan followed Brown to the lee side of the poop deck. The captain's quarters were forbidden territory to all except those invited.

The two men made their way below deck. The ship reeked of bilge water and rotting timber. Proceeding down the dimly lit, narrow corridors, Morgan noted a door ajar. Muffled cries drifted from beneath the entrance.

"Don't mind the noise," Brown barked. "You get used to whiny women." Pausing at the end of the corridor, he rapped softly on a second door. "You in there, Elliot?"

A gravel voice returned. "That you again, Brown?"

"Open up. I've got someone with me."

The door opened a crack and a pair of rum-sodden eyes peered out. "You bring another woman?"

"No, I'm here on business. Let me in, Elliot."

"Business? Now?"

"Just open the door."

Weathered oak swung wide to reveal a disheveled, dirty man who was well into his cups. Brown entered the stinking cabin, motioning Morgan to follow.

The captain viewed the intruders with a wary eye. "Who do you have with you?"

"Dov Lanigan."

"Dov Lanigan!" Elliot's eyes narrowed as he lifted a shoulder to wipe his runny nose. "What's going on? I thought we were supposed to meet Lanigan in New Orleans."

"We were, but a stroke of good fortune has brought Mr. Lanigan to Galveston this evening. Now make yourself presentable for Mr. Lanigan."

Lifting a bottle of rum to his lips, the captain eyed Morgan briefly before he took a hearty swallow. Grunting, he said. "State your business, Brown." Wiping the back of his hand across his mouth, he wove his way toward his bed.

"We've come for the woman."

Lying back on his bunk, Elliot raised his hand to block the light from the one small candle. He squinted. "Dov Lanigan, huh?"

Brown heaved an impatient sigh. "I believe I've made the proper introductions."

"Odd, don't you think? Lanigan showing up here is a tad suspicious?"

Brown shrugged. "I admit it was a bit of a surprise to me. But here he is. Big as life."

"How can you be so sure he's who he says he is? I hear Lanigan sticks real close to New Orleans. A price on his head and all."

"My dear captain," Brown replied, "may I remind you that all of us have a price on our heads?"

The captain leaned unsteadily on one elbow "Yeah, well, the reason no man has had the good fortune to claim the reward for my dead body is because I'm just a wee bit on the cautious side." The captain slapped the lumpy mattress beneath him. A puff of dust rose from the filthy coverlet, and a large cockroach sprang to the floor and darted in Brown's direction. "I'm not a fool." The roach scurried several inches before a dagger sliced the air and split its back, nailing it to the wooden floor.

Brown and the captain focused in stupefied silence as the roach's legs pumped furiously for an instant, going nowhere. The legs halted abruptly and then stilled.

Morgan kept his expression neutral as he pulled his dagger out of the plank and met the two men's eyes. The captain drew his legs up as Morgan reached for the filthy blanket at the foot of the cot and slowly wiped both sides of the blade before inspecting it.

Candlelight glinted off the beveled blade but did not penetrate Morgan's shadowed eyes as he turned it slowly, lovingly with nimble fingers. He then silently slipped the weapon into its sheath. Brown cleared his throat.

"Mr. Lanigan, you're quite handy with that thing." Brown glanced at the captain. "I hope the matter of his identity is settled to your satisfaction."

The captain grunted and swung his feet to the floor. The expression on the man's face left no doubt that his pride was injured. "What do you want from me?" He pushed himself to his feet, more alert now.

"Take me to the woman." Morgan used a demanding tone and an uncompromising stare.

Brown turned diplomat. "I'm sure Dov

wants to see for himself if the lady is as beautiful as I've claimed her to be."

"Which one? There's a bunch of 'em. You want the older one? The youngest?"

"The latest one. Brought her here not two hours ago."

"Women come and go here like flies." The captain appeared to be taking Morgan's measure. "All right. No harm in lookin'." He gestured toward the door. "Long as you remember not to touch till she's paid for."

Brown turned. "I think Mr. Lanigan knows the rules better than we, Captain."

Moments later, two robust seamen appeared on deck, dragging between them a fighting, spitting Amelia.

"Let go of me, you miserable, smelly brute!" Her teeth sank into the hand of the man restraining her, inciting a string of oaths that fouled the already putrid air.

The sailor glanced to Brown pleadingly. "Let me teach this one a lesson. She's a bloody handful, she is! My pay ain't worth puttin' up with this blooming persecution!"

Jerking the bodice of her dress into place, Amelia glared at the lout threatening her. With a toss of her head, she turned her attention to Brown.

Morgan sensed that she was preparing to tell him where to go and how quick to do it when she recognized who was standing beside Brown.

Her jaw dropped. "You . . . !" she sputtered.

Mr. Brown smiled. "Watch your language, dear. My friend, Lanigan, will think you're a hooligan."

"Lanigan? Lanigan, the privateer who was reputed to be merciless with a knife?" Morgan Kane was the notorious Lanigan? She shook her head in disbelief. The nightmare wouldn't end.

"Ah, this one seems to have spirit," Morgan, or rather, *Lanigan* observed. "Highly spirited. I appreciate all that fire and bluster."

Beaming now, Brown nodded. "I thought you would."

Amelia twisted and pulled until her breath heaved in gasps. With exasperated oaths, the men on either side hauled her arms behind her to force her cooperation. "You low-down, dirty, thieving snakes in the grass!" Amelia screeched, focusing on Morgan. "How dare you take advantage of me this way?"

A slow smile spread across the man's features. "Yes, she's full of spit and vinegar."

Her eyes pinned him to the spot. "You, sir, should do some soul-searching. Maybe you'll find one."

Turning away, Lanigan said in a bored tone, "Will someone stop her tiresome prattle?"

"Listen, you!" Amelia's eyes shot fire at her swindler. "You get me off this ship and do it right now or I'll —"

His sharp glance halted her intended threat. He wasn't Dov Lanigan — she'd bet her life on it — but why was he pretending to be the disreputable privateer? But she couldn't give his identity away if she had the slightest hope of getting out of this bad dream. There must be some sort of plan behind his brazen hoax. He was the only ticket she and the other women had to leave this boat.

Lanigan dismissed her with a sullen glance. "I don't know about this one. Perhaps she's not worth the cost. Perhaps she's touched with madness."

"No, no," Brown assured. "She is quite intelligent. She'll bring a pretty penny if you decide not to keep her."

With helpless rage, Amelia pooled a mouthful of spit and hurled it at Morgan Kane.

Stiffening, he appeared to rein his anger. If looks could kill, she would be lying dead at his feet right now.

She spat again. "You no-good swine." She spat a third time.

"Stop spitting on me."

She spat again.

Mr. Brown stepped over to wipe the spittle off Lanigan's coat. She spat on Brown.

"See here! You stop this!" Brown demanded. "Do you know whom you're spitting on?"

Amelia's eyes fixed accusingly on Morgan, but she kept silent, working up more spit in her mouth.

"The woman is a lunatic." Morgan . . . Lanigan jumped back when she spat again.

Mr. Brown snapped his fingers, and two seamen stepped forward to stuff a dirty rag into her mouth.

She kicked and clawed, trying to spit out the vile-tasting rag. The men bound her tightly with a rope, laughing at her struggle.

Lanigan circled her slowly, appraising her like a prize horse. Up and down, her eyes followed his, promising revenge.

"She is pure?"

Brown nodded. "Of course . . . pure as the driven snow."

"Is there a doctor aboard?"

"Certainly," Brown replied. "Of course, there's the little matter of his license being revoked, but when he's sober, he knows his business well enough."

"I will expect her to be as pure as an angel," Lanigan warned.

"She will be examined immediately, but I can assure you this one is rare."

Lanigan's gaze met Amelia's smugly. "Good. She will think twice before she spits on men again."

"Take her below," Mr. Brown ordered.

Amelia's eyes widened when the two seamen proceeded to drag her away. Examined? What was "examined"?

Turning to Morgan, Brown apologized. "I'm sorry you had to witness that bit of unpleasantness. She is a bit high strung, but her mind is completely intact, and as you can see, her beauty is unsurpassed."

Morgan knew Amelia McDougal would be mad as hops when she returned. But in order for him to save her life, she would be forced to prove her value.

"I will take the other women too."

"The others? Why, there's as many as —"

"Doesn't matter. Have them ready to leave within the hour."

"Sir, this was not the plan. Do you have the cash? And there is the matter of delivery fee."

"The money will be in your hand tomor-

88

row morning. I will make arrangements to have the funds delivered to the ship early. Don't sail before the runner arrives."

"Well . . . the request is highly unusual . . ."

Morgan pinpointed Brown's gaze. "Are you questioning my word?"

"Oh no! No, sir! Morning will be fine. The earlier the better." The men turned to leave when a shuffle erupted between Amelia and two seamen. She drew back and kicked one in the shin. A string of oaths colored the air.

The man raised a fist, and Morgan's arm shot out. "Leave her be! She belongs to me."

"But she's —"

"Leave her!" Kane's voice ricocheted off the water.

The seaman dropped his arm, but the second thug tightened his hold on the struggling girl.

Amelia shrugged free, straightening her posture. "I can *walk,* thank you."

Brown cleared his throat. "Your ship is nearby, Mr. Lanigan? I can provide you with excellent quarters . . . and many hours of pleasant diversion."

"No, as soon as the women are ready, we'll be leaving." Morgan prayed God would provide a way to carry on the ruse until early tide. There was the small problem of locating a ship to house who knew how many other women. Had he lost his wits? Assuming responsibility for lives he'd never met. He'd be responsible for their safety, feeding and housing them, and keeping them from the clutches of Dov Lanigan.

The answer was yes. Apparently he had lost his wits, and it didn't appear likely that he'd find them anytime soon.

Now all he had to do was find a boatload of money, get a ship, rescue the women, and stay on mission.

Amelia sucked in fresh air when she emerged from the bowels of the ship, cheeks aflame. If Morgan Kane was still aboard, he'd be living the last few minutes of his contemptible life. She had never felt such consummate hatred for one person. When the doctor took her below and performed . . . she closed her eyes as humiliation burned her cheeks. Proving her purity was the most demeaning travesty she'd ever encountered. It was bad enough that the captain of her dreams defrauded her, but how could he call himself a man?

And yet something deep inside her trusted this man. Undoubtedly, word had spread about another conquest for Dov Lanigan, and Morgan was there to save her from an unspeakable fate — one more daft blunder because of her neglect.

As much as she longed to throttle the captain, she would do or say anything needed to play along with his deception until she could catch a moment alone with him and demand to know how he knew where she was and how he planned to save her and a boatload of women from certain ruin. The odds were monstrous against such a daring rescue. Freeing her was one matter, but rescuing eleven women was quite another matter.

If Kane was willing and able to do all this, she would literally owe this man her life.

When Morgan stepped outside on the deck, he saw light flare as a young woman struck a match with her thumbnail and lit the cigarette dangling indolently from her lips. Her gaze locked brazenly with his as she slowly removed the cigarette and held the match just below her face. The light cast a flattering glow on her strong cheekbones, her straight nose, her arched brows. Her lips puckered in a provocative pout before she blew out the match. In the sudden darkness, her eyes held his for an instant before he turned and strode toward the railing. She spoke first.

"Go ahead, say it. I'm a fool."

Drawing her to a sheltered alcove, he chanced a second look to see if anyone witnessed the exchange. The deckhands were too absorbed in bringing the women on deck to notice the captain. "You're far from a fool, Elizabeth, but you were incredibly careless. How did you end up here?"

"How do you think? Like the others, I was captured by Brown's thugs. The question is, how did you know I was here?"

"I didn't." Morgan struck a match, his eyes locked with hers. He touched the fire to the tip of her cigarette.

Inhaling deeply, she shook her head. "We're in serious trouble, aren't we?"

"I think we can safely assume that we are."

She brought the smoke back to her mouth. "I don't know what happened. I wasn't careless. One moment I was walking along, minding my business, and the next moment I was overpowered by two burly thugs who dragged me to this diabolical hole. In the blink of an eye, I found myself a prisoner of Austin Brown, a despicable soul who plans to sell me and the others."

"It does boggle the mind, doesn't it?" Morgan focused on the silent harbor. "Have any idea where we can buy a ship?"

"Buy one?"

"Temporarily borrow one."

"That's crazy, Morgan. We don't have funds to buy a ship. Let's just get out of here."

"Desperate times call for desperate measures. There must be some sloop or freighter in the harbor unattended."

"You're serious. You plan to go through with this ruse — take these women and run?"

"That's my plan."

"It's insane. We save ourselves." Drawing on the cigarette, Elizabeth appeared to consider the idea. "Taking the others will be too dangerous — is it true you actually know the McDougal girl?"

"Briefly. We met on the trail. She was in trouble then, but nothing like this."

"She claims she's met you. You're willing to lose the mission and possibly get ourselves killed to come to her assistance a second time?"

"Are you suggesting that our job is less dangerous?"

"Listen." Elizabeth turned pleading eyes on him. "I'm sorry I let down my guard —"

"No need for apologies. We've worked together long enough to know that neither of us would intentionally endanger the other. The circumstances were unforeseen, I can't deny that, but there is a way out. I just have to find it."

"It better be clever. I trust you more than any agent I have worked with, but the situation is so grave, I have to wonder how any of us could survive unharmed."

"The task isn't enviable, granted. The situation developed so fast, I haven't had time to devise a plan. I overheard Brown bragging about your capture in a pub, or I wouldn't have known what happened to you. I came for the McDougal woman."

"The featherhead? You're here because of the featherhead?"

"She's smart enough, Elizabeth. There are times when she doesn't use her best judgment, but she knows her limits."

Elizabeth took a step back. "You're *defending* her. In the brief time that you've known her, you've appointed yourself her protector? The girl will get us killed with her reckless and impulsive nature."

"She's young and impressionable," he disputed.

"Pigheaded and brash!"

"Childlike and inexperienced," he dismissed.

Elizabeth stepped closer. "Why are you shielding her? If it wasn't for her, our lives wouldn't be in danger."

"Amelia might well have saved your life. Calm down. I'll get us out of this."

"So a child inadvertently led you to me," Elizabeth repeated. "What about the mission? This could destroy all we've accomplished. We are so close to seizing Lanigan. So close!"

"Consider this a stroke of unbelievable luck. The mission is intact. We know for certain where Lanigan is now. No more wild goose chases to locate him only to lose him again."

"Sheer madness," she murmured. "Surely every man aboard this ship has seen or met Dov Lanigan —"

"They haven't. I know it sounds unbelievable, but from what I've heard, Lanigan doesn't show himself often. It does sound unlikely that not one packet rack would have met him, but that appears to be the case. Even Brown is buying the charade — for the time being. If anyone knows Dov Lanigan, they haven't spoken up. We take our chances. Unless you have a better idea."

Elizabeth discarded the cigarette and ground it out on the deck with her heel.

"Hey," Morgan chided. "What will our host think of your treating his ship with so little esteem?"

"Frankly, I don't care what the captain thinks."

"For the moment, I'd suggest you be more courteous and play the helpless captive." His gaze shifted to the empty deck. "You never know when ears are listening."

Elizabeth appeared to calm. "In the meantime, what do you want me to do?"

Morgan answered as candidly as he could. "I have no idea. I'm making this up as I go, but I won't leave you and the others here."

"Of course not. Morgan Kane always puts others first."

"I wouldn't leave a wild boar here."

"There are over fifty men aboard ship . . . against the two of us. The situation is hopeless."

"Ah, but there will be twelve of us, and nothing is ever hopeless. But I'll need your full cooperation."

"My help? I'm a prisoner. Remember?"

"Play it smart, and do as Brown tells you. The voyage to Houston will be short, provided the weather holds. By the time we get there, I'll have a plan."

"We're going to Houston?"

"For the time being. We have to get out of Galveston immediately."

"You'll have a ship, I trust."

"I will by the time we need one."

"What about the squirrel? Shouldn't she be told we're working together?"

"No," Morgan said flatly. "Amelia is not to know about our association. The less she knows, the better."

"Now there's a ray of light. She's clueless —"

"Elizabeth —"

"If she knew we're working together, she might show more caution."

"Tempting thought, but false. Like I said, she's young and naive."

"Ah! Then you agree with me. She's an anchor around our neck!"

"Charmingly impetuous," he maintained.

"You just met the woman! What is this fascination with her?"

Morgan said quietly, "We have enough trouble without inviting more. The girl can be dealt with, Elizabeth." His voice turned grave. "I don't need to warn you that you and Amelia are fighting for your lives. This is not the time for backbiting and petty bickering —"

Elizabeth straightened. "You said your misplaced sense of responsibility for Amelia McDougal was born because you rescued her from a jail wagon, but I don't have the same passion, Morgan. Far from it. The woman is dangerous — not only to us but most definitely to our mission.

"I understand, but this isn't the time for heroics," Morgan warned. "These men have no soul. None. You would do well to remember it. If Amelia knows nothing about our association, she can't arouse suspicion among anyone we encounter."

"You're serious? You really don't plan to inform her about our association?"

"Not a word, and I strongly advise that you use the same common sense."

A weary sigh escaped the woman. "I'm scared. There was a time when life held no meaning for me, but it isn't that way anymore. When the war's over, there's so much I want to experience, so much living to catch up on. I can't bear to think that a mere child like Amelia would hold the key to my future."

"Nobody has any keys, Elizabeth. But the women have God and a fairly formidable couple of experienced government spies on their side. That was enough for Joshua in the battle of Jericho; it should be good enough for them." Morgan's thoughts wandered back through the years when he had sat at his grandmother's feet as she read the Old Testament aloud to him, recounting the battles and struggles God's people had faced. The accounts had stuck with him.

So Joshua arose, and all the people of war, to go up against Ai: and Joshua chose out thirty thousand mighty men of valour, and sent them away by night. And he commanded them, saying, Behold, ye shall lie in wait against the city, even behind the city: go not very far from the city, but be ye all ready: And I, and all the people that are with me, will approach unto the city: and it shall come to pass, when they come out against us, as at the first, that we will flee before them, (For they will come out after us) till we have drawn them from the city; for they will say, They flee before us, as at the first: therefore we will flee before them. Then ye shall rise up from the ambush, and seize upon the city: for the LORD your God will deliver it into your hand. And it shall be, when ye have taken the city, that ye shall set the city on fire: according to the commandment of the LORD shall ye do. See, I have commanded you.

"Maybe, but God had His eye on Joshua," Elizabeth whispered, breaking Morgan's thoughts.

Morgan shook his head. "God hasn't changed. If we keep our heads and God is with us, we can outwit these hooligans. Lay low and follow my lead." He met her eyes in the flickering light of whalebone lanterns swaying from the yardarms. "I have a hunch we're in for a rough ride."

FIVE

The remaining captives were manhandled onto deck. Morgan stood by as brawny seamen silenced fearful cries with the backs of their hands. The exchange appeared to be little more than a cattle roundup. A man shoved Amelia across the deck, drawing back to strike her in a silent warning.

Amelia glanced in Morgan's direction and discreetly eased to the shadows. He had no doubt her thoughts toward him were none too charitable. The purity examination was the only way he could get her off the ship. Each captive had to endure one.

Minutes passed as he watched the women gather. Suddenly he felt a cold blade in his side.

"You're upset," he observed dryly, knowing without doubt who the assailant was, but puzzled. How did Amelia get a weapon? Her grudge was likely to get them killed.

"You low-down, cross-eyed weasel." She

pressed closer to his ear. "I'm going to slit your gullet and then saw your serpent tongue out of your scheming, two-faced, ugly head."

"Would it offend you if I asked why?"

The knife slowly lifted to his temple. "Do you know what an 'examination' is?"

"Where did you get the knife?"

"I *stole* it."

He calmly bent to search his boot holder. "Easy now," he warned when the blade cut lightly into his throat. He straightened. "How did you get my knife?"

"I told you. I'm good. Now say your prayers, heathen."

"All right, but I'm your only hope of getting off this boat."

"You're not the least bit worried about me. You're with these thugs."

"Believe what you want, but I'm not here for my health."

"How did you know where I was?"

"Overheard Brown bragging in the tavern."

"I don't believe you."

"Your choice."

Her tone assumed a note of grim finality. "If you have any last words, you'd better say them."

"You're going to be sorry."

"You let me worry —"

He whirled and took the knife so fast she blinked. "Are you out of your mind?" He tucked the blade in his boot.

She rubbed her wrists. "I told you my intentions."

Taking her arm, he pulled her to the front of the boat, into the shadows. "You're endangering every woman on this ship. Now listen and listen close. I'm only going to say this once. I am not Dov Lanigan. I said I was in order to save your hide."

Her lips pursed suspiciously. "Then who are you?"

"Exactly who I said I am. Morgan Kane."

She eyed him warily. "Who are you really? No more games, because I know my imprudence and hard head has landed us squarely in the boiling pot this time."

"My name is Morgan Kane. For now, that's all you need to know."

"How could you have possibly known I was here? And the others?"

"I told you. I overheard your new friend, Austin Brown, bragging in a pub about his conquest. I had no idea what I would find when I got here — certainly not a boatload of kidnapped women."

Amelia groaned. "How foolish can one woman be? What can I do? I don't want to be *sold* like a side of beef!"

Dazed and frightened women roamed the deck. The noise was deafening, but Morgan realized they had talked too long. Suspicions would be aroused. He turned as if to leave, his voice carrying softly over his shoulder. "For now, I want you to continue the role of the victim. That shouldn't be hard for you."

"Keep it up, mister. I could change my mind and still cause you great bodily harm," she whispered.

He paused. "Ever the victim."

"I *am* the victim!"

"Go where you're told, as if you were resigned to your fate."

"And what do you plan to do?"

"You let me worry about that." His gaze skimmed the rowdy privateers gleefully bedeviling the women. And worry he would until he had the situation in hand.

And this thorn in his side, Amelia, on her way back to Mercy Flats.

The moon had slid behind a cloud bank when Morgan gripped the knife handle in his teeth and dove off the pier into the cool water. With strong, sure strokes, he swam for the ship tethered at the farthest slip of the long pier. The less-than-seaworthy-looking vessel concerned him, but the ship was afloat. For the time being, the craft fit his need.

Amelia and Elizabeth waited with the other women in a deserted warehouse while he secured the vessel. According to loose tongues, the crusty old sailor who owned the ship would do anything for enough money. The three-mast barque was a disgrace to its owner, but that only made Morgan's job easier. A few coins should secure the women's passage to Houston.

When he reached the boat, nothing stirred. Apparently the owner was in a sound sleep or intoxicated state. From this distance, Morgan could hear snores resonating from the deck. The old ship rocked back and forth, its boards creaking like aging bones in the light wind.

Silently slipping aboard, Morgan crept toward the dim light filtering from the half-closed hatch. His hand closed more tightly around the blade handle as he gently, slowly reached for the opening. A hand clamped on his shoulder.

"Looking for somethin', matey?"

He whirled to confront a grizzled man with white whiskers and rum-soaked eyes. The knife blade flashed in the half-moon. *I can take him if needed.* But he'd rather not.

Violence wasn't on the agenda. "I need your ship."

"That a fact?" The fellow took a swing and grazed Morgan's cheek. Morgan pinned the man's arm to his hip. "Relax. I am here to bargain with you."

"If you're going to slit me throat, do it quickly."

"I mean you no harm. I work for the United States government, and I need your help. If I release you and you don't put up a ruckus, I'll show you my credentials."

The old man grunted and met his gaze. After brief thought, he said, "Are you giving me a choice?"

"That's up to you. We can handle this in a civilized manner or beat each other's brains out. I'd prefer the first."

The old sea captain's stance slackened, and Morgan gradually relaxed his hold. In seconds, he produced a loose paper.

The old man shook his head. "Put your papers away. I cain't read."

"Shall I read it for you?"

"Just tell me what you need."

"I need your ship temporarily."

"This old tub?"

"Sorry, sir. You will be compensated." Morgan sized up the older man, more confident the old sailor was going to be reasonable. "How large is your crew?"

"What crew? I don't have a crew. Look around, mate. Who in their right mind would work aboard this vessel?"

Relief swept Morgan when he realized the man wasn't going to fight for the vessel. A fistfight wasn't in the plan. "How much?"

The old man squinted. "How much? Well, I think she's worth every bit of, say, twenty coins."

"Twenty." Morgan frowned. He wasn't carrying that amount, but he could send for the money if the old man agreed.

The man stepped closer. "What was you thinking?"

"I only need the ship for a day or two. Twenty coins is fair."

"I can't pay a cent more than twenty. The government can put that in their pipe and smoke it." The old man crossed his arms.

When his words registered, Morgan said, "No. I asked what I could pay you. What is your fee to lease the craft?"

"*Pay* me? Money? Are you accusing me of being a thief? I've been trying to rid me-self of this hangnail for years!" The old man made a valiant sweep of his hand. "You're welcome to it!"

Morgan's heart sank. Apparently he'd picked the only worthless vessel in port.

"How many will she hold?"

The man's eyes narrowed as though he thought Kane was daft. "She's been rammed by a whale once when I was sailing in the Pacific. Tore her up pretty good. Then a couple of hurricanes roughed her up —"

"How many?" Time was wasting. The women would think he'd deserted them. He frowned. "Is she seaworthy? No holes in her hull?"

The captain's gaze dropped. "None that comes to mind."

"You wouldn't lie to me, would you?" He needed a ship, not a leaking tub.

"Got her here, didn't I?" The old man removed his hat and scratched a bed of lice, unless Morgan was mistaken. "How many are you talking about?"

"Eleven. Women. All women. I need to transport them to Houston tonight."

His eyes widened. "A tad overdoing it, ain't ya?"

"They're not my women. I'm *escorting* eleven females."

"Oh. Well, she holds seven at best. M'lady would hold a lot more, but she's starting to sag in a few places. Females might fall through rotting timber. Got a few weak spots here and there."

"Will she stay afloat?"

He drew back. "Of course she will! I said she was sagging, not rubbish."

The ship was rubbish but apparently his lady now. The price would go up. "She'll hold seven? Four more isn't going to hurt, is it?"

The old man scratched thick whiskers. "Suppose not — they'd have to sleep on deck. Every one of 'em."

"That'll do. Will you accept a promissory note from the government?"

"To buy the ship?"

Morgan didn't need a sloop. "I'd prefer not to own it, but I have to get the women out of Galveston tonight."

The old man's hand shot up in protest. "You take the boat. She's yours — I don't want her back."

Morgan didn't have time to argue. "How much food is on board?"

"Couple of tins of sardines, some moldy hardtack."

Morgan mentally counted his funds. There was enough to provide food for the brief trip.

"I'll need your help. While I get the women aboard, you gather enough food to last through tomorrow. Cheese, sardines, crackers, fresh fruit. We'll need fresh water. Can you do this?"

The old man nodded. "I can. If you provide the funds and promise to keep the boat. Fresh water's no problem. There's a deep well nearby."

Morgan needed a run-down ship about as much as he needed another female, but time was short. He would deal with the matter once they reached Houston.

"Good. As long as we're in agreement. I'll get the women."

The only good thing Morgan could find about the unexpected turn was that Amelia, in her naïveté, had led him straight to the crux of his mission. Capture and arrest Dov Lanigan. Selling women for profit wasn't Lanigan's only crime. He was gunrunning for the South, and the government wanted him. Elizabeth and Morgan had been sent to nail him.

If it weren't for the soft spot in his heart for anyone serving the Lord, he would have — should have ridden right past that jail wagon of nuns.

Amelia huddled in the drafty warehouse with her back pressed to the wall. A cool wind blew off the water and cut through her cloak. The less-than-honorable Austin Brown had provided no comfort for his captives. Most of the women had only thin sleeves to protect them from the biting cold. Brown's expression had shown no hint of compassion. Only greed dominated his features when the exchange was made. The women filed by, and he absently rubbed his hands together, no doubt anticipating the windfall soon to come his way. Little did he know he was being played for a sucker.

"What's taking him so long?" someone whispered.

"He'll be back." A shiver raced down Amelia's spine. He *had* to come back.

"How can you be certain?" Pilar, one of the young captives, shook her head. "It seems we're in worse trouble than we were, if possible."

Amelia bit her lower lip, pulling her cloak closer. She longed to spill the beans, but she couldn't. Though she would like to smack Morgan upside the noggin, she would play along with his plan because she must. She wasn't dumb, and she valued her life — plus she would never do anything to further endanger the other ladies' lives.

"I don't know about y'all, but I'm going to pray." Mahalia, the dark-skinned one, started, and the others bowed their heads. The young lady's voice swelled with pleas. "Loving Father, take this unspeakable evil and turn it for Your good —"

The heavy door slid back, and Morgan, accompanied by an older gent, appeared carrying an armload of blankets. "Put these around you."

Amelia gratefully accepted a covering "Did you find a ship?"

"I found something close. It will have to do." He turned to face the women. "All right, ladies. You can set your fears to rest. I am not Dov Lanigan."

Soft, surprised exclamations broke out.

"My name is Morgan Kane — Captain Morgan Kane. I am with the United States government. For now, that's all you need to know about me. Rest assured that I'm here to rescue you — if that's possible." His gaze slid to Elizabeth, who looked visibly relieved, and then continued addressing the group. "I'll need your full cooperation to pull this off. My plan, for the moment, is to get you out of Galveston, which doesn't mean you will escape harm. The hoax will buy you time — how much I can't promise."

Excited chatter broke out, and he raised his hand to silence the women. "Celebration comes later, if there is a later. I know there are a hundred questions racing through your minds about me and about your future, but we're playing this by the minute. Time is fleeting. Don't speak a word, and stay in the shadows. The ship to freedom is located at the end of the dock. Board swiftly. We can't risk the chance that Brown will catch on to the ruse before we set sail. If we all row, we can move the vessel offshore and go undetected before early tide."

The women's heads bobbed with relieved acceptance.

"Let's go. Stay close and no theatrics. You're safer in a group than trying an escape on your own."

One by one, the women filed out of the shed, hugging the shadows. Boisterous laughter filled the air even at this late hour. Seaman were drinking themselves into a stupor before staggering back to their ships before dawn.

An old vessel bobbed in the water at the end of the pier. The strong smell of rotting fish filled Amelia's nostrils as she kept pace in line. Captain Kane was taking a huge risk. The departure was yet another delay in his plans, and once again she was at fault. Guilt washed over her. The whole unsettling matter must test his patience to the limit. When was she going to stop following her impulses, which inevitably proved mistaken? Long ago she had grown tired of scamming others. Why hadn't she stopped then instead of waiting for another foresee-able disaster?

Dearest God, if You will only get me out of this situation alive, I promise to never take from another what isn't mine. And whether Abigail likes it or not, she might just find a man like Captain Kane and like him. Yes, really like him, maybe even marry the man and have more children than the stars . . .

Well, maybe not the stars, but a bunch.

With her heart in her throat, she kept to the shadows, turning to shush an occasional suppressed sob. Once, the entourage was forced to pause as two men exited a tavern. The packet rats appeared to take little notice of the strange line of women on their silent march to the port.

Amelia focused on the vessel moored at the end of the pier, and her pulse quickened. *Please, God, just a few more steps . . .*

A white-haired man with a surprisingly strong grip grasped her hand and helped her aboard. One by one, the women stepped lightly. Embarking took less time than to fry an egg. Morgan turned and hauled up the plank before he addressed the women. "Ladies, if any among you is a praying woman, I would suggest you be about it. The tide is still a few hours away. Until we set sail, we won't be safe. Even then, Brown will most likely discover the swindle and follow us."

"Where are you taking us?" Bunny asked.

"Captain Frost," he nodded to the older man, "assures me he can get us safely to Houston. From there, you'll be on your own."

"But I live here," Ria said.

Another joined in. "So do I!"

"Me too!"

Morgan lifted a hand. "I'm sorry for the inconvenience, but we must leave port. I can only get you as far as Houston. From there, you will have to make arrangements to return." He glanced at Elizabeth. "I know this is not to anyone's liking, but I can't leave you to Brown's mercy. He doesn't have any."

"I have no funds for return passage," Pilar said.

Morgan looked to the old captain. "Perhaps you can help the women find return passage? I will provide the funds."

"If you got enough money, I can do anything," Frost said.

"Then it's settled. Once we reach Houston, we scatter." Morgan's gaze swept the women, pausing to rest on Amelia. "Don't test my patience. I am at the end of my rope."

He turned to face the women. "Sorry for the conditions, but it's the best I could come up with on short notice. You will sleep on deck. The weather is mild, and the captain assures me he has more blankets. With a brisk wind, we'll be in Houston by midafternoon tomorrow."

Amelia's gaze swept her deplorable surroundings. Rotting deck. Dirt everywhere she looked. Grime and filth. She winced when she spotted a rat scurrying under a moldy plank.

She didn't know about the others, but she didn't intend to ask for an additional blanket, and she certainly wouldn't be getting much sleep.

Dawn slowly lifted a veil of foggy mist off the emerald waters. Amelia drew a deep breath of briny air and admired what promised to be a glorious sunrise. The sky was magnificent today above the dazzling gulf. She felt wonderful this morning even though she hadn't closed her eyes once. She had never been on a ship, never experienced the delight of listening to water slap against the hull as the sloop skimmed over mildly choppy waves.

Overhead, seagulls dipped and swayed in a dizzying array, and twice she spotted playful dolphins leaping in and out of the water. Truly, she would never forget this frightening yet invigorating experience. Was it possible that Abigail and Anne-Marie might be having the times of their lives? Or had they met an unspeakable fate? Shaking the thought away, she focused on the sheer beauty of the moment. Soon she would be home, reunited with her sisters. She wouldn't allow her thoughts to drift otherwise.

"Beautiful, isn't it?"

Amelia glanced up to see Pilar resting her forearms on the railing beside her. The young girl's eyes were so lifeless, the sight brought heaviness to an otherwise splendid day. One so young should have luminous eyes and a bright smile, but Pilar had neither.

Morgan Kane had once again come to the rescue, and shortly she and the other women would have their freedom. She had never considered how precious freedom was or the high price mankind paid for the privilege. Morgan was taking a huge risk by his selfless effort to save her and the others, in addition to serving his country. The awful conflict that she'd hardly witnessed came into sharp focus when she recalled the rows of displaced people roaming the back roads with small children, their worldly belongings strapped to their backs. What a selfish child she had been just a week ago. Her circumstances were dire, but she couldn't help but wonder if God had not set her on this strange journey in order to learn. But what? The true meaning of life? Of how one person could make a difference? In this case that person would be Morgan Kane, a righteous man.

She acknowledged Pilar's presence. "Where are the others?"

"They're at the front of the ship watching dolphins. The creatures are charming, aren't they?"

"Quite. I could watch them all day." Amelia shuddered, her gaze tracing the dirty deck. "How can Captain Frost live in these conditions?"

Pilar's brow rose. "Have you noticed his appearance?"

The wind battered the women's unencumbered hair as they stood at the railing, watching the sunrise. If it weren't for the gravity of the situation, Amelia might wish the day would never end. Her fears were diminished with Morgan aboard, but the almost certainty that Brown would soon discover the ruse hung heavy in the back of her mind. No one could know when he would have discovered the deception, but she'd be willing to concede that he hadn't gotten where he was by being naive or foolish.

"Why don't we move up front and join the others?" Amelia was developing a motherly fondness for the young women even though she was not much older than most of them. Overnight she had learned the girls' names. Pilar, the one with sorrowful eyes. Elizabeth, the shrew. Auria, quiet and frightened. Belicia, the girl she found sobbing on her bunk yesterday. Ria, who laughed a lot, though she had no reason to. Mira, the girl who smiled through her tears. Bunny. Dark-skinned Mahalia. Faith and Hester.

Sighing, Pilar leaned closer to the railing, eyes fixed on the water. "Everyone is frightened out of their minds. Most of us have nowhere to go once we reach Houston."

"Frightened of what? We are in most capable hands now."

"Brown and his men. They're dreadful animals." Pilar's gaze focused on the waves breaking against the hull. "I don't know Morgan Kane. For all we know, he could be even worse than Brown."

"Oh no. He isn't. I know him."

Pilar turned to meet her gaze.

"I do know him. He rescued me from a jail wagon a few days ago."

Pilar's jaw dropped.

"I wasn't in the wagon for anything serious. My sisters and I helped ourselves to a few pieces of fruit — the apples were soft and the oranges were tough skinned. We didn't take the best — but anyway, you can rest assured that Morgan Kane is an honorable man."

"But how . . . ?"

"It's a very long story, but please don't be afraid. Morgan will do all that he can to save us. You have my promise. We need to concentrate on what you and the others will do once we reach port. Brown *will* follow. He is greedy and spiteful and won't let us go easily, but neither will Morgan." She wasn't the fool Elizabeth accused her of being. Brown would never let the women get away without a horrendous fight.

Pilar frowned. "You would think Brown would be smarter than to fall for the trick. Surely he couldn't think that this Dov Lanigan would just sail in and take the women on his own."

"Obviously, Théodore Austin Brown isn't as smart as he thinks."

120

Pilar slowly shook her head. "You might be confident this Morgan Kane will bring us through this, but I'm not convinced. You're pretty and smart and probably have someone who is waiting for you when this is over. Most of us have none of those things."

"Rubbish. I'm not the least bit smart, but yes, I do have somewhere to go after this is over." The mission nuns must be peering out windows and listening intently for the three McDougal sisters to return. It wasn't unheard of for the ambitious girls to wander for a few days, but they always came home by the end of the week.

"Anyone have a better plan than Kane's?" A new voice entered the conversation.

Amelia turned to discover that Elizabeth and Bunny had decided to join them. Elizabeth issued the brusque challenge.

"Pardon?"

"You may be a ninny, but for once you're right. We are far from out of this yet. This isn't a child's game. We do what Kane says without hesitation."

Bunny nodded in agreement. "I would rather be killed trying to escape than hand my life to a heartless privateer."

Amelia stiffened at Elizabeth's combined compliment and insult, but she held her tongue, agreeing the group had bigger problems than choice of words. Elizabeth possessed common sense, though she abused the attribute often. From the moment Amelia laid eyes on her, steel barriers had shot up, and she wasn't sure why. Maybe Elizabeth's overbearing, bossy nature crowded her sunnier side. Amelia hoped to be done with her soon.

Bunny sensed the tension and continued. "There's strength in numbers. No one should act alone. Regardless of how frightened we are, we must consider the other first."

Amelia's eyes locked in a silent duel with Elizabeth's. "I agree."

"See, we can be in agreement when we try." Bunny smiled. "My concern is what to do when once we arrive in Houston. I don't have a coin to my name. How will I find my way back to Galveston?"

Amelia reached for the girl's hand. "Must you return there?"

"Well . . . no, I suppose not. I was living on the streets when Brown captured me. My husband took ill and died a couple of months ago. I had nowhere to go and didn't know what to do. I've been living on handouts."

Amelia had discovered that many of the

women told the same story. No families. Alone and helpless — easy prey for those like Brown and his cutthroats.

"We can't permit our thoughts to dwell on the unknown. We'll deal with problems as they arise. We need to pray for wisdom and guidance. When Brown discovers the hoax, no doubt he will try to recover his losses, but by then we will be long gone." Hope was their only defense. Without it, they would most certainly be lost. "I know the situation looks bad, but if we put our heads together, we can come up with something."

Most of the women clearly did not share the same optimism.

"Why don't we just burst into a round of song?" Elizabeth mocked.

Amelia pointed at her. "If you listen to her, we might as well slit our throats and be through with the ordeal. Life is full of trials. We'll face whatever comes our way."

Bunny's eyes widened with distress. "I don't want to slit my throat."

"Only a figure of speech." Amelia gave the girl's shoulder a reassuring pat. "Please don't worry. Of course the situation is grave, and I'm not making light of our distress, but we must keep heart. To lose confidence is exactly what these rats want, and we will *not* give them the pleasure of seeing our vulnerability."

"Well, then. Do tell us what to do," Elizabeth said.

"I think we have agreed to follow Morgan Kane's orders. Do exactly as he asks."

Elizabeth shook her head. "Twit."

Drawing herself up straighter, Amelia faced her accuser. "If you think name-calling will hurt my feelings, you are sadly mistaken."

"My, my." Elizabeth rolled a smoke. "Sounds like someone is infatuated with the handsome young captain."

"Infatuated!" Amelia felt steam roll from the top of her head.

"Quiet!" Pilar snapped. "Stop this endless squabbling." She glanced at Elizabeth. "Captain Kane is taking a huge risk — one he didn't invite. Of course we'll do as he says."

Elizabeth ignited a match with her thumb. The woman took a long drag off the cigarette. Bold, she was. Blatantly brazen.

"Can we please not argue?" Bunny stepped to the rail and took a long draught of fresh air. "Can't we just thank God that for now we're unharmed? Surely we can figure a way out of this." She closed her eyes and took another long, deep breath of sea air.

Silence turned deafening. Elizabeth flipped the cigarette overboard. Red-hot ashes swirled into the wind. "This day is never going to end."

The woman was not only haughty, but she was wishy-washy. One minute she was hot on a plan and the next she seemed oblivious to danger. Sister Louise said wishy-washy was worse than indecisive. Make a point and stick with it, the good sister said. Elizabeth would have been well served to have a Sister Louise in her life. Tears welled in Amelia's eyes. How she wished the gentle, kind sister was here right now to advise them all.

Elizabeth suddenly stepped back and shoved Amelia against the railing. "Listen, and listen good, silly twit." Elizabeth was so close that Amelia could see the flecks of gold rimming the pupils of her eyes. "Stay alert."

Amelia gave her a cold stare. "Let go of me."

Elizabeth straightened, releasing the bruising hold. "Use your head for more than a hat rack."

Amelia had heard that plenty of times before.

"Our heads, Elizabeth, are not our immediate concern." Amelia irritably straightened her disheveled bodice.

Casting a glance at Captain Kane, who was standing in deep conversation with Frost, Elizabeth added quietly, "Just keep quiet and do what you're told."

"Speak for yourself, gooseneck." Amelia's hand flew to cover her mouth. The mission sisters would take her to the woodshed for using such language. *Blessed are the peacemakers.* How many times had the beatitude been drilled into her? "Elizabeth . . ."

Turning on her heel, Elizabeth walked off, no doubt leaving the other women to wonder about the pulsing dislike between the two women.

Six

The hours passed slowly. The ship's old captain said that with a good wind the sloop could do eleven knots. But the wind had calmed to little more than a stiff breeze. When Amelia wasn't lying on deck staring at the sky, she was pacing the deck, staring at the miles of endless water. The sea fascinated her. She could stand forever, watching the dolphins frolic in the water like playful children on a school holiday. Her thoughts turned to the end of what had been promised a short journey. By late afternoon they would be in the subport of Houston, Morgan had told her, though nobody informed the wind of their goal. The old ship cut through waters as thick as molasses now.

But she was in no hurry. Once in Houston, her adventure would be over. A worrisome sense of regret filled her. The past few days had covered the full array of emotions. Fear, anticipation, hope. Standing at the ship's rail, feeling the breeze toss her hair, she no longer felt like the old Amelia. How would life at the convent ever satisfy after this whirlwind venture?

"Still watching the dolphins, Miss McDougal?"

Expectancy fired Amelia's blood as Morgan approached. He had an unnerving effect on her, and she suspected the other women felt the undercurrent. She saw the glancing looks, the wistful stares. Even Elizabeth appeared at times to be taken by his presence.

"They're delightful to watch. So carefree. So unrestricted."

Overhead, the wind snapped through the fore and aft sails as the old vessel sliced silently through the water.

"Are you worried?" he asked.

"Me?" She chuckled. "Heavens, no." At least if she were, he'd never know it. She had been very selfish, imposing upon his time with hardly a thought for his schedule. She would not cause him one more minute of trouble.

Settling his weight against the spray rail, he studied her. "You've been avoiding me all day."

"I have not. I've rested, watched the sea.

Besides, you've looked quite busy all day."

Light swells struck the bow of the ship, mesmerizing Amelia. The sea was calm and peaceful. The past few days were almost forgotten amid such beauty. God's hand was evident everywhere she looked. The formation of the clouds, the deep waters, the sea life — magnificent work. With those things, combined with Morgan's presence, she felt at peace. She was developing far too much dependence on this man. Very soon he would ride on to his mission, and she would book passage to Mercy Flats. Something cavernous inside her recoiled from the thought. She didn't want him to leave. The foreign thought left her mystified.

Before she realized it, she blurted, "Do you find Elizabeth to be nice?"

"Elizabeth?" he replied vaguely.

Elizabeth? she mocked silently. He knew perfectly well who Elizabeth was. She was rough, crass, and foulmouthed, but she was pretty with that mass of dark hair and sea-green eyes. Of course he'd noticed her. "Yes, Elizabeth. Do you think she's nice — and pretty?"

"Elizabeth with the gorgeous eyes?"

"The woman with the gorgeous eyes." Ha!

His tone was noncommittal. "Haven't noticed her." A slow grin spread over his

129

face. "Why do you ask?"

Amelia deliberately kept her tone sunny. "I don't care, but you should know she's hateful." That remark was even more unkind than calling her a gooseneck. Elizabeth's neck was quite pretty, long and slender.

He nodded. "But very attractive."

Amelia sucked in a breath. "Can't deny the truth. She's pretty hateful." She turned on him. "You have noticed her."

The dimple appeared.

Amelia had heard of such instant attractions — a man and a woman, their eyes meeting across the room, feeling a sense of destiny. The thought that the good Lord had destined Morgan Kane for Elizabeth made her queasy.

"That's it, isn't it?" she challenged.

"That's what?"

"Mutual attraction. I've seen the way you two step into the shadows to whisper." Drawing her cloak closer, she struggled against the inexplicable feelings suddenly battering her. Was jealousy rearing its ugly head? Sister Lucille had warned her about the serpent's ugly ways, but why would it pick this time and, most especially, this man to torture her? She didn't care who Captain Kane looked at with longing eyes. She rigorously jerked her wrap tighter.

"What were you and the others so deep in conversation about earlier?" Morgan asked.

"Freedom."

A dangerous light entered his eyes. "Freedom is within sight. Use the opportunity wisely."

"I didn't say I was going to do anything silly, but if I were you, I would keep an eye on . . ." She bit back another odious remark. She had no right to tattle on Elizabeth. He'd understand her and her petty ways soon enough. She wasn't capable of taking orders, not from a man like Kane, who wouldn't put up with her nonsense.

"On whom?"

"Never mind. I would just be cautious of whom I trust."

"You are not to do anything foolish," he repeated. "When we reach Houston, you will be a free woman. Go home."

"Well, thank you. I *will.*" She picked an imaginary speck of lint from her cloak.

"And don't try anything daring. Your headstrong devices are what got you into this in the first place."

"My reasoning has always worked for me in the past." Though she hated the tactics. She'd never realized how much until this journey. She longed for a simple life, one free of strife. One with a husband like Kane.

One who looked like him but didn't act like him. She'd been a pest, and he rightfully would be happy to be rid of her. She, on the other hand, would not be so thrilled to watch him ride away. If circumstances were different . . . She dropped the idea.

"Just follow my advice. Buy a train ticket —"

"There are no trains near Mercy Flats."

"Then ship."

"Mercy Flats is a long way from a deep port, but I will buy ship passage."

"Stagecoach?"

"Same story. But rest assured, I will return to my home and my sisters." She turned to meet his gaze. "What about you? Where will you go when we reach Houston?"

Silence, as though he were considering a thought. Then, "The less you know, the better. Just follow instructions."

"In other words, I'm to follow along like a gullible dolt, and all will be well."

"I didn't say that. We're a long way from completing this little escape."

"But you seem so . . . confident."

"I'm not. Deep down, I'm praying as hard as the others. If this idea backfires, I'm afraid it will be every man for himself. I cannot keep eleven women safe, not even remotely."

"But you brought the other women."

"Forget it," he said sharply, as if he'd already given the subject considerable thought. "As much as I'd like to, I can't save them all. I'll only take one when I leave."

"Oh, let me guess who that will be."

He focused on the water, declining the challenge.

When she could stand the suspense no longer, she erupted with the name that she'd come to despise. "Elizabeth," she noted. "It's Elizabeth, isn't it?" Her head swung away. "You're disgusting."

"I don't make a habit of discussing my ladies with other women. I learned a long time ago that I might as well cut my own throat if I venture there."

Her features hardened with determination. She wasn't exactly on firm footing right now. She wanted his attention, but not like this. Turning, she walked away, tossing over her shoulder, "How much longer to Houston?"

"Can't say. You in a hurry to get there?"

"No, gooseneck."

"Gooseneck? What's that supposed to mean?"

Swiping hair from her eyes, she muttered under her breath. If he thought for one moment that he and Elizabeth's obvious attraction bothered her, then he was a gooseneck.

If she was headed for the woodshed, she might as well make the painful trip worthwhile.

The sun sank below a wall of clouds as the ship approached Houston. The hour of deliverance had finally arrived. Soon she would be home, reunited with Abigail, Anne-Marie, and the sisters at San Miguel. How worried those lovely nuns must be. The McDougal sisters had been gone . . . well, she'd lost track of time, but longer than usual and certainly enough to worry the nuns into a frenzy.

The sloop slipped silently into the harbor. Straining to see through the murky haze, she tried to detect movement on the outer bank. There was none.

A foghorn sounded in the distance, signaling an approaching ship. Houston was a subport, unable to handle huge vessels, but the sloop easily anchored into place.

"See anything?" Ria pressed closer to Amelia's side, her body trembling with anticipation. Captain Frost, a cautious sort, had moored the vessel a safe distance from the landing, no doubt to avoid detection. A thick gray mist hung low over the port and couldn't have come at a better time. The stench of the waterfront met her nose.

"The fog is so thick, I can't see my hand in front of my face." Amelia's eyes located Elizabeth's and challenged her. Did she know Morgan planned to take her with him and leave the others behind if trouble arose? An envious twinge drew her back to the present.

The low, melodious call of a songbird came from somewhere near the shoreline. Pressing against the railing, Amelia listened more intently. There it was again, two owl hoots followed by a seagull call, stronger this time.

"That's the signal," she murmured. "We have to go now." Fear nearly blocked her air passage. However much comfort she found in Morgan, she realized he could only do so much. Her life would depend mainly on her efforts to survive. She was a strong swimmer, had known how since she was a sprout, so the short swim didn't alarm her.

The women drew closer, fear evident in their whispers.

"Stay close together," Amelia said. "If we're discovered, don't stop. Run as fast as you can. Escape by whatever means you find. From this moment on, we're basically on our own."

The women, with the exception of Elizabeth, paused to give a reassuring group hug. Amelia's thoughts swirled. In the brief time they had been together, she had begun to have real affection for Ria and Mahalia. She would miss them dreadfully. She broke the embrace and took a deep breath. "We have to swim to shore."

Elizabeth approached the waiting group. "Can everyone swim?"

Heads nodded affirmatively, but Bunny flinched. "It's so chilly. The water will be miserable."

Elizabeth closed her hand around Amelia's arm and pulled her aside. "Get out of the way. If you're not going to lead, I will."

Amelia met Elizabeth's eyes — black and hard, exactly like her heart — and stiffened with resentment. Wrenching free from the bruising hold, Amelia stood her ground, refusing to be bullied. "Be my guest." This woman was not going to bully her ashore. She would go under her own power.

Pilar took control of Amelia while Bunny got a firm hold on Elizabeth. The two women separated the warring parties.

"You can settle this later." Ria motioned to follow her.

Elizabeth jerked free, stepped onto the

railing, and grabbed for a rope dangling from the mast. Pushing off, she shimmied down the hemp and dropped silently into the water.

Drawing a fortifying breath, Amelia braced for the cold swim. "Ready, ladies?" Slipping over the side of the ship proved to be exhilarating, and the steep drop snatched Amelia's breath.

Pilar's voice sounded lost and small on deck. "Promise to stay close to me?"

"I won't leave your side. Try to be brave!" Cold water enveloped Amelia, and she lost sight of the ship temporarily when her head went under. Bobbing to the surface, she shuddered. The water was freezing!

One by one the women grabbed hold of the rope and eased down the steep side of the sloop. Amelia heard soft gasps when each hit the water, but the girls immediately took breaths and dove under.

Pilar splashed over to Amelia and clung to her hand tightly, her eyes wide with fear.

"Don't be afraid," Amelia whispered. "It's not far to the bank."

"I can't swim," Pilar gasped.

"You can't swim? But when Captain Kane asked —"

Pilar's whisper was laced with panic. "I fibbed — I didn't want you to leave me behind."

Amelia grasped the girl tighter and pulled her along behind her.

When they reached the bank, one by one the women surfaced, panting for breath. Amelia and Pilar followed in the distance, their heads bobbing above the water.

Morgan appeared, parting the grass that grew thick along the small inlet, as Elizabeth climbed out of the water and immediately established a stance beside him. "You have a knack for picking women, Kane." She dropped to the grass, breathing heavily.

Morgan grunted. "If you're referring to Amelia, I didn't pick her. But for curiosity's sake, what's she done now?"

Elizabeth gave him a dark look.

Amelia witnessed the hurried exchange, and her heart broke. The moment Elizabeth had reached shore, she'd gone straight to Morgan. Regaining her senses, Amelia realized that she was foolish to throw caution to the wind, no matter how angry Elizabeth made her.

Amelia grasped Pilar's hand tighter, and the two women struggled to their feet and walked out of the water. One by one others emerged and huddled close, shivering in the chilly dawn.

Morgan paused, his gaze skimming the empty pier. He gathered the group in a huddle. "The area is swarming with war activity. Any more than two traveling together will be certain to draw attention. Keep to the shadows and get as far from the water as possible before sunup." He met Amelia's expectant gaze. "I would take you farther, but my job will not allow me." His tone softened. "Be careful and . . . Godspeed."

A shout came from a nearby ship and an alarm sounded. A small schooner now sat in the bay. One glance and Amelia saw men running on the decks, pulling on clothes as they ran. As suspected, Brown had figured out he'd been swindled and had followed. An overcast sky had prevented the steam-powered boat from being detected until daybreak.

Morgan noticed a light frantically swaying back and forth from the old ship they'd left. Frost wanted Morgan to take ownership of the vessel.

Amelia stepped closer. "Morgan, I think Captain Frost is trying to get your attention."

"I see him."

"What does he want?"

"You ask too many questions. Go!" Morgan, with Elizabeth following on his heels, set off in a dead run, heading south. Frost had been paid a fair wage; it would be up to him to rid himself of that flea trap.

The women scrambled, sidestepping a scurrying armadillo as the animal fled into the underbrush.

Morgan's boots pounded the ground, putting distance between him and the ship. He had miscalculated the situation. Brown had either discovered the ruse or suspected foul play and followed the sloop. The thug had put two and two together and come up with another detriment to threaten Morgan's mission. Other than Elizabeth, Morgan had no one but himself to look after. The thought wasn't comforting. He was not a man to leave a helpless woman — in this case, ten women.

Amelia crossed his mind, and he experienced an odd sense of betrayal. He'd deserted Amelia and the other helpless females who had little hope of survival.

He stopped short, breathing heavily. Elizabeth raced past him, skidding to a halt fifty feet away. She bent, both hands on her knees as she caught her breath. "What?"

"I can't leave them."

"Morgan! Have you lost your mind! We have to save our own necks — we have no other choice!"

"There's always a choice, Elizabeth. Good or bad."

"Going back is bad. Unthinkable. We have a job to do. Now let's get it done and go home."

"If you want to go, leave with my blessing. I'll assume responsibility, but I think we can complete our mission and save those young women without the government ever knowing about our small detour from the plan."

Elizabeth dropped to the ground, panting. "Does she mean that much to you?"

"Who?"

"Amelia."

"I'm not thinking about Amelia. She's capable of caring for herself." The woman was too adept. She and her two sisters should be Southern spies.

"Sorry to inform you, but the little twit stole your heart when you weren't looking."

"You're talking gibberish. What kind of man would I be if I left ten women to Austin Brown's mercy? Chances are, he won't sell the women to Lanigan now. Brown's been made a fool, and he wouldn't want Dov Lanigan to get wind of his blunder."

"Morgan, we have Lanigan in sight. We know with certainty he's in New Orleans and likely to stay there until his bounty is delivered. Lanigan might not get the women, but someone will. Brown won't free the urchins regardless. He'll sell them to yet another despicable man for profit. If we move quickly, we have Lanigan and we go home. There's no way to move quickly with ten women in our hair." She paused. "And unless you've forgotten, I've sworn my loyalty to my country. And so have you."

"Everything you say is true, but those women have no one but us to help them."

Elizabeth rose to her feet. "You've lost your mind, you know."

"Clearly."

"The women have scattered like chaff. We'll never find them."

"You are most likely right. I couldn't be happier if that were true."

"But we're going to try anyway. Right?"

"Right."

Morgan got to his feet, and his eye caught movement in the shadows. He drew his firearm. "Who goes there!"

Amelia meekly stepped from the shadows, followed by Pilar, Auria, Belicia, Ria, Mira, Bunny, Mahalia, Faith, and Hester. The women paused in front of the captain, heads bent low.

"You?"

"Yes, sir." Amelia's chin touched her chest.

Elizabeth threw up her hands and stepped back.

Morgan turned stern. "Is this your idea of running?"

"We have been running, sir."

"Behind me and Elizabeth."

"You said run. You didn't specify in what direction."

He glanced at Elizabeth, who rolled her eyes. "Your call, *Captain* Kane."

The decision was an abandonment of his duty, and Morgan knew it, but the war and his duties would pass. His conscience would not, and Elizabeth would never turn him in for misconduct. He turned to address the group. "Listen and try to follow orders. We run until we can't run any longer. Does everyone understand?"

"With you?" Bunny asked. "We can run with you?"

"With me . . . and Elizabeth." His eyes shifted to Amelia. "You. You run beside me like I'm your second skin. Understood?"

"Yes, sir. Where are we running to?"

"Beats me." He didn't trust her impulsive nature, yet he didn't care to lose his life. Nor did he care to risk his mission. For now,

he had ten women in his hair. And Elizabeth.

There was always Elizabeth.

When the party was winded, Captain Kane
paused and knelt on his haunches to draw a
crude map in the loose dirt with his forefinger. There had been no sign of Brown or his
crew. By the time the thugs departed their
ship, Morgan's group had a sizable lead on
the buccaneers. The women huddled close
as Kane explained the next step.

"Roughly forty-five minutes away is the
Mississippi Lady. Like the sloop, it's old but
serviceable. The captain is a personal friend.
If we can make it to the boat, Jean Louis
will take us to New Orleans. I hope." His
and Jean Louis's friendship had been long
and loyal, but Morgan had never asked
anything like what he was about to ask from
Jean Louis. Loyalty and friendship might
just fly out the window with the bizarre
request. "That means my friend will have to
detour to the Jacinto River down to the Gulf
and go east to the Mississippi. But with
God's grace I think we can count on his
help." He glanced at Elizabeth, hoping she
had caught the emphasis he'd put on New
Orleans. The delay would not be a delay.
The team was still squarely on a mission —

to capture Dov Lanigan.

His tone assumed a note of gravity. "Ladies, you have two choices. You can split up here and try to make it back to your families alone, or you can remain together, and hopefully I'll get you to New Orleans." New Orleans, Memphis, Galveston, Houston, and now back to New Orleans. They were running in circles. He hadn't spoken with Jean Louis in months, but he knew his friend's schedule. The captain carried iron from Houston to seaports on a regular basis. All Morgan needed was prayer, cooperative weather, and the grit to get the women to the *Mississippi Lady. God, please let Jean Louis be between runs and agree to the unconventional plan.* All were long shots, but Morgan was out of choices.

"Another captain? How are you acquainted with this captain?" Amelia countered.

"Does it matter?"

"To me it does. What if he's another Austin Brown or someone even worse —"

"You have my word, he is reputable."

Elizabeth appeared to consider the thought. "New Orleans?"

"New Orleans," Morgan confirmed, meeting her eyes.

"We still have the quandary on where we'll

go once we reach New Orleans." Auria spoke this time.

"Let's take one problem at a time. Let's just get to New Orleans, if we can."

Pilar edged closer to Amelia, her young body visibly quaking. The women, shivering in the damp air, looked to one another for answers.

Turning back to the women, Amelia asked softly, "What do you want to do? We could try to make it on our own. It will be difficult, if not impossible. We have no money or knowledge of the area. We could always seek shelter with the church in New Orleans if we have to."

Because of the war, the church shelters were overcrowded in both Houston and New Orleans.

Pilar said quietly, "At this point, does it matter?"

Amelia reached for Bunny's and Belicia's hands. "No. We stay together."

Rising, Morgan nodded. "Move quickly. No doubt Austin Brown is on our heels — or will be soon."

A light mist dampened their barely dry clothing by the time the women reached the *Mississippi Lady.* Parting the thick undergrowth, Amelia peered at the tall paddle wheelers tied side by side at the wharf. She was old but looked to be well cared for.

A young black boy sat atop a bale of hay playing a harmonica while gangs of roust-abouts loaded bales of cotton onto the decks of steamers headed downriver. Along the banks, men lifted trunks and carpetbags from horse-drawn wagons onto the low main deck of a steamer about to depart.

Men's voices singing a happy tune granted the only warmth to the unseasonably cool day.

"Stay together," Morgan warned.

Amelia smothered a grin. He needn't have worried. He couldn't have scraped the women off his side with a bowie knife. Motioning for the group to follow, Morgan started for the gangplank.

Bunny stepped into the lead, followed by Amelia, Pilar, Hester, Faith, Ria, Mahalia, Belicia, Auria, Mira, and Elizabeth. One by one, the women marched in a long row to the vessel, looking neither right nor left.

As they crossed the gangplank, Amelia held her breath against the stench of oily, hot boilers. Her eyes took in the iron cargo and firewood strewn about on the old deck. Moving closer to Morgan, she whispered, "The boat looks safe enough." Her eyes fixed on the boiler on the main deck. "But if that thing blows up, we'll be flung clean back to Houston."

"I imagine you're right, but I've never had that experience, and I visit Jean Louis often."

A distinguished white-haired gentleman dressed in a blue jacket and wearing a captain's hat appeared on deck, a smile spreading across his amiable features as the entourage approached.

"Well, well. Morgan Kane, a sight for sore eyes." The captain of the *Mississippi Lady* walked down the plank, and the two men embraced warmly. When they parted, Jean Louis broke into an even wider smile. "And Elizabeth! What a treat!"

"You're looking good, my friend." Elizabeth shook his hand.

"Can't say that my regrets outweigh my blessings."

Drawing the captain aside, Morgan explained the circumstances. The captain's face turned pensive. His eyes traveled the line of women.

Morgan turned and made hasty introductions. "Ladies, this is the captain of the *Mississippi Lady,* Jean Louis Matter."

Captain Matter, a man perhaps ten years older than Morgan, perused the women closely. "Some of them are little more than children, my friend."

Morgan explained the peculiar circumstances before he turned to Amelia. "And this is Amelia." He flashed a grin that made Amelia's heart flip. "The one who started this distraction."

"Ah. Such a lovely diversion." The captain paused, his eyes searching the young woman's.

"I'm Pilar." A girl's words broke into the awkward silence. Then the other women added their names in turn. Auria, Belicia, Ria, Mira, Bunny, Mahalia, Hester, Faith.

Captain Matter returned the greetings. "Well, as Morgan knows, I carry only cargo. Iron and cotton, mostly." His eyes centered on the empty lower deck. "But it would seem you're in luck. I made my last run recently and don't plan another until next month. I can't offer anything fancy, just good food and a place to rest your head during the week's trip, providing the weather holds."

Compared to the sloop, the *Mississippi Lady* was a floating palace. Amelia spoke up. "Captain, we aren't in a position to be choosy. Your help will be most appreciated."

"I'll do all I can, but the journey won't be without a fair share of risk," he promised.

Morgan's eyes grimly beheld the women.

149

"We'd appreciate any help you can give us."

"My crew is old and the quarters are very small. But . . ." A crafty smile touched the corners of the captain's eyes. "With Morgan aboard, we can still outsmart anyone on the river."

Morgan glanced over his shoulder. "You can bet Austin Brown isn't going to be far behind."

"Then we'd best be underway. Most likely we don't have a minute to spare." Captain Matter signaled to the pilothouse, and a moment later the steamboat's warning bell clanged.

An old man, stooped and balding, lifted a Chinese gong and shouted, "All aboard that ain't going get off the boat!"

Within a short time, the gangplank was drawn in, and the *Mississippi Lady*'s engine roared to life with a rhythmic *chaukety-paw, chaukety-paw, chaukety-paw.* A shout went up as plumes of black smoke sprinkled with sparks poured from the old paddle wheeler's stacks.

Amelia hung over the railing in anticipation, watching a rush of water appear between the hull and the shoreline as the old packet slowly turned to the stream, pointing its bow toward the Jacinto River.

The decks vibrated beneath her, and she

drew a long, heady breath, wondering if she'd ever see her sisters, the convent, or Mercy Flats again.

Please let it be, Father. I not only love each one dearly, but I can't wait to tell them of my adventure! Oh, and about Morgan Kane. Not that he's that important, but he is . . . special. Please guard his steps in order that he can get us all to safety.

As Captain Jean Louis had promised, the quarters were small. The women were assigned five to a cabin on the lower deck. As the eleventh woman, Amelia agreed to alternate sleeping between the two cabins, although it would make for crowded conditions. The women agreed there was safety in numbers, so no one minded the inconvenience.

The *Mississippi Lady,* though far from spotless, was worlds better than the sloop, which among other things had seaweed and marine life crusted on the hull. The paddle wheeler's interior looked as if someone sought to keep the space orderly but couldn't quite achieve the goal. The women went immediately to their quarters, reeling from their exhausting flight. They'd been under way only a short time when an interesting-looking elderly gentleman wearing thick eyeglasses delivered food to the cramped quarters.

Tipping his frayed nautical cap, the old man bared a row of overly large buckteeth. Sister Agnes would say he could eat grass through a picket fence. " 'Enry Muller's the name, and you'll be safe as a chick in her mama's nest with us," he promised. He dished out plates, tin cups, and bountiful portions of the tasty fare that looked to be seafood chowder. The smell of hot biscuits and fried apples made Amelia faint with hunger. They'd eaten sparely, and the thought of a hot meal made her heady.

"How far to New Orleans?" she asked as she gratefully accepted the coffee the stranger was pouring from a large black-and-white splattered porcelain pot. By this time, she was hungry enough to eat or drink anything anyone offered.

"At least a week," Enry conceded. "But the water's good!" He grinned, showing lots of big teeth. "Once we're on the Mississippi, other than an occasional planter or sleeper, we shouldn't have any trouble."

"What's a 'planter or sleeper'?"

"Well now, I can see you little girls have a lot to learn." Enry heaped a couple of extra biscuits brimming with butter on Amelia's plate. "I'm talking about snags in the river, trees, logs, driftwood . . . things like that."

Amelia took a sip from the steaming cup, trying not to stare at him. She didn't want him to think she was staring at his teeth. She wasn't. It was just hard not to. They were large. Really big.

"Is there someplace we could wash our dresses?" Pilar asked.

"Sure is! There's a tub of rainwater just down the deck." He flashed another toothy grin. "Just help yourself."

Pilar sat up straighter. "Do you have soap?"

"Made a fresh batch this morning. Lye, goat's milk. Good stuff. I don't tell the others what I put in it, but they like it. I have all you need."

After they'd eaten, the women gathered at the rain barrel to wash. Enry brought several large bars of soap and a stack of thin hemp towels. The girls chattered as they scrubbed their hair and their muddy clothes. As far as Amelia was concerned, this boat was heaven compared to the sloop. Her thoughts drifted to the moment they had boarded the *Mississippi Lady.* Captain Jean Louis greeted Elizabeth warmly, even called her by name. How did he know Elizabeth?

The association made no sense. What was Morgan trying to hide? Or Elizabeth? She couldn't possibly know Captain Morgan Kane. She had been a captive, the same as Amelia. Morgan had no reason to disassociate himself from Elizabeth because of Amelia. The three were complete strangers a few days earlier.

She made a mental note to speak to Morgan about the confusing relationship the moment she could find a minute of privacy with him.

Morgan sat in the wheelhouse with his childhood friend, listening to the women splash. Captain Jean Louis smiled as the female giggles filled the air.

Shaking his head, the Frenchman tapped tobacco into the bowl of his meerschaum pipe. "Got yourself a handful, my friend. How do you do it?"

Morgan's gaze unwillingly fixed on Amelia, watching as she vigorously scrubbed her hair with a bar of soap. As she rinsed away the lather, the fiery highlights in the long strands glinted in the sunshine. Earlier clouds had cleared, and the day turned out to be sunny and warm. Amelia slowly tossed her head, and her tresses fanned out over her shoulders.

"Now that one's a rare jewel," Jean Louis said.

"She's a real spitfire." Morgan shook his head. He resented the feelings Amelia McDougal aroused in him. And the idea both pained and intrigued him. She was the first woman he'd met that actually matched him wit for wit. Every encounter with her strengthened his resolve to know her better. He was actually starting to consider the hour she left for Mercy Flats. Eventually the day must come. Had this been a different time in his life, he might be of mind to explore this childlike woman and discover the real Amelia McDougal, but that was futile thinking. The war raged on, and he owed his duty to the government.

"Say you rescued her from a band of Comanche?" Over dinner Morgan had told his friend about the events of the past few days and how he came to have the lovely Amelia in his care at the most inopportune time.

"Since Elizabeth's with you, I assume you are on a mission."

"I am." Jean Louis knew Morgan never spoke about his business, so the turn of conversation was brief.

"What was a lovely one like Amelia doing in a jail wagon?"

Turning away, Morgan centered his interest on the passing scenery. "You would have to know Amelia, Jean Louis. She tends to draw trouble like a watermelon does flies."

"I take it you have a plan once you get the women to New Orleans?"

"None. I was hoping you might have a suggestion."

"Ten women?" Jean Louis shook his head. "Right now I can't think of a thing, except maybe take the youngest ones to an orphanage or church mission. Even at that, they're a mite old."

"One of the reasons I wanted to take only Elizabeth with me. The women's circumstances aren't the best, but neither are mine. I have little time to dally before my subject will move on. The man has slipped through my fingers more than once. I know exactly where he is now, and I don't intend to lose him again."

"You said some of the ladies were homeless when they were abducted?"

"Some were. Amelia said one or two of the younger ones have families to return to, but the older ones had been living on the streets."

The captain shook his head. "Pity. This dastardly war has changed lives forever."

It was more than a misfortune. Morgan's gaze returned to the women. Kidnapping was a crime, one he felt powerless to do anything about.

"Once we reach New Orleans, they'll be on their own. Because I assumed responsibility for Amelia, I've promised to see that she is returned to Mercy Flats, but the others will need to look after themselves. I don't like it, but circumstances leave me no other choice."

"Except for Elizabeth." Jean Louis looked on him kindly.

"Elizabeth and I work together, Jean Louis. Not by choice."

"Work together, eh?" His friend chuckled. "You two have been together for years, and she's still nothing more than a working partner?"

"Nothing more. And that goes for both sides." Over the years Morgan had developed a distinct fondness for the woman, but love wasn't involved. Elizabeth felt the same about him. They made a good team, but the interests of both lay elsewhere. "I don't need to remind you that we are speaking in strict confidence."

Jean Louis chuckled. "Spying seems a mighty risky business for a woman."

"Elizabeth is as smart as any man I've met. She's had some hard knocks in her life brought on by her willful ways. She stays to herself, does her job, and doesn't take anything off of anybody. I admire the woman, though I admit that I don't like her much."

"That right? She married?"

"Not anymore."

"Uh-huh," the captain mused. "That bad?"

"I haven't asked the details and don't plan to. It seems marriage left a bad taste in her mouth."

Jean Louis shook his head. "I would have wagered that the two of you were very close."

Morgan chuckled. "Elizabeth and I are misleading the others about our relationship because of the nature of our business. You should have that figured out."

"Even Amelia?"

"Most assuredly, Amelia."

"Now, what's the point in that? Aggravating a bunch of females doesn't seem like your style, friend."

"Life's simpler that way." Morgan knew whatever he confided with his friend would go no further. The same could not be said of Amelia. "Elizabeth and I are on a mission." He grinned. "But you're welcome to court her the brief time we're aboard, friend."

"You'd do that to me?" The captain chuckled.

"She could have a gentle side, but I've yet to come across it. She can out-cuss a sailor, fight like a boxer, and nag a man to his grave."

"My dream of the perfect woman," Jean Louis noted.

Morgan's eyes lifted. "I haven't mentioned it, but once this mission is over, I'm going to be excused from service for a brief time."

The captain's eyebrows arched in surprise. "Why?"

"Silas is near death now. Laura can't work the orchards alone anymore. If we can believe the rumors, the war could be over soon. If so, I will be free to leave. I've served my country, Jean Louis." Turning away, he finished softly. "Laura needs me, and Elizabeth has a strong case of wanderlust."

"Pity. But I know your deep affection for Silas and your Aunt Laura. Your mother — have you seen her over the years?"

Morgan shook his head. "I heard she's still alive somewhere in California."

"Well, maybe some women aren't cut out for motherhood."

"Laura and Silas are the only family I've known. Without their grace, I'd have been living on the streets at a very young age."

He'd always figured that he would marry and settle down, but he hadn't planned on meeting "his lady" for many years. Perhaps that was why Amelia disturbed him. He wasn't ready to meet a woman like her.

She in no way bore a resemblance to the woman in his mind. She was pretty enough, but she kept his insides tied in a knot most of the time. Circumstances would change. Amelia would go her way and he would go his, and this nonsense he was starting to feel every time he was around her would evaporate.

"It wouldn't hurt to settle down in the meantime," Jean Louis offered, as though he'd read Morgan's thoughts.

"You have my promise." Morgan flashed a grin. "I will the day you do."

The men's gaze strayed back to the laughing women. "Ah," Jean Louis said. "Is there anything lovelier than a woman's beauty and allure?"

"Not much." The agreement might be mutual, but Morgan hated to think that the woman, smelling of soap, with the sun glinting off the red streaks in her hair, had any permanent hold on his life.

She didn't. He'd make sure to guard the growing temptation.

Seven

Amelia was the first up the next morning. Dawn streaked the sky with bright orange and red when she left Pilar still asleep and climbed the few steps to the deck. Red sky at night, sailors' delight. Red sky in the morning, sailors take warning. The old-timers would say they were in for a storm today. To her relief, the temperature was warm. The old paddle wheeler gently churned the muddy Mississippi, making its way slowly upstream.

Taking a deep breath of fresh air, she smiled as she headed straight for the cook shack, located between the decks and the storeroom. She felt more optimistic this morning, and when she was optimistic, she was hungry. If the food was anything like yesterday, the trip would be even more pleasurable. The bacon she'd eaten all these years paled in comparison with the meals the cook put out.

The smell of coffee and frying bacon encircled her as she climbed the steps to the galley. She hadn't tasted bacon since she'd left the convent.

She paused, her gaze skimming the railing. Morgan wasn't on deck, though she was certain he was around. He rose earlier than chickens. Elizabeth wasn't anywhere to be seen either. Amelia followed her nose to the galley. What did Morgan see in Elizabeth that she didn't? He could hear her harsh tone, see her callous manner. And those dreadful cigarettes. Her clothes smelled of smoke, and the inside of her right forefinger was stained with tar.

Sister Mary Grace at the convent would make Amelia say a ton of Hail Marys for such uncharitable thoughts, but she longed to shake Elizabeth and then ground out the tobacco on Captain Jean Louis's deck. She wasn't a pretty woman in the normal sense; her mouth was a tad bit too large, and her complexion had pockmarks from lack of care, but her eyes and the way her nose tilted just slightly to the right could charm a man. But what man would want to kiss a smokestack?

Correcting her attitude, Amelia reminded herself that she didn't care if Morgan favored Elizabeth. And even if she did, she had no right to question the man's taste in women. She would think a man like the captain would prefer a sweet-smelling, soft-spoken, kindhearted lady, but if he was attracted to a shrew, a ruffian with a salty tongue, then Elizabeth was an ideal choice.

Amelia tapped on the galley door and smiled when it opened to reveal an elderly woman. Everyone on this boat looked old.

"Good morning," Amelia greeted. "The bacon smelled so good, I thought I might snitch a piece."

The old woman looked as tough as a twenty-five-cent steak. "You did, did you?" she said in a gravelly voice.

"Yes, ma'am." Amelia widened the smile, hoping the woman would reciprocate. She hadn't met the cook yesterday — only eaten the fine food she produced from the big black woodstove.

Leaving her standing in the doorway, the lady returned to the huge frying pan of sizzling bacon.

Without waiting for an invitation, which obviously wasn't coming, Amelia entered the galley. "I'm Amelia."

After reaching for a slice of bacon draining on the sideboard, Amelia casually lifted herself onto the counter, making herself at home. She had spent hours in the mission kitchen, whiling away the time with the sisters. The nuns hadn't seemed to mind, and Amelia had nothing better to do, so she'd talked for hours about anything and everything that interested her, which included anything and everything.

She was reaching for another slice of bacon but jerked her hand back swiftly when the cook threatened to swat her with a wooden spoon.

"Got a whole boatload to feed, ya know."

"Sorry," Amelia replied sheepishly, "but it looks like you have plenty." There must have been three or four pounds of bacon set to drain.

The old woman shuffled to the counter and began to crack eggs into a large bowl. "Name's Izzy. This here's my galley, and don't you forget it."

"Yes, ma'am, I won't. Want some help?"

"If I'd wanted help, I'd have asked."

"Yes, ma'am." Amelia eyed the bacon speculatively.

Throwing a pinch of salt in the pot of beans boiling on the stove, Izzy fixed on her. "Don't you have nothin' better to occupy your time?"

"Nary a thing." Sliding off the counter, she gave the old woman a gentle nudge aside. "Let me help you."

The cook shrugged, moving to the oven to check on a pan of biscuits.

"You're old, aren't you?" Amelia cracked an egg and frowned when part of the shell dropped into the bowl.

Izzy lifted the bacon out of the skillet with her right hand, her left hand resting on her hip. "Your momma never teach you no manners?"

"I don't mean any disrespect. It's just that you look pretty old." Amelia knew that she was often thought to be younger than she was, so she didn't see any problem in asking. If you didn't ask, how would you ever know anything? She'd always wished that she'd looked older, and she imagined the old woman probably wished she looked younger. No one was ever satisfied. "My mother left me and my sisters at a Catholic mission when we were very young. The good sisters have tried to teach us proper upbringing, but I'll admit the McDougal sisters were born with a wild streak. Of course, our true mother couldn't have known that, since she abandoned us so young, but the note she left tucked in my blanket said she could no longer afford to feed us and she was going to look for work." Amelia sighed. "She must've not found anything, because she never came back."

She glanced at the bacon. "Is it all right if I eat my two pieces of bacon now? I promise I won't take more when breakfast is served."

A smile threatened the old woman features. "Yes, I'm old, and you can take two pieces. No more."

Grinning, Amelia reached for a strip of the delectable pork. "How old?"

"How old do you think I am?"

Amelia thought that this woman looked older than dirt, but she wasn't about to say so. Sister Agnes looked older than dirt, and she was seventy-two. Frightfully old.

"Well, maybe seventy and a half?"

Izzy dipped flour into the skillet and thickened the drippings for gravy. She chuckled. "Now that's mighty kind of you."

"Older than seventy and a half?"

"If you must know, I'm ninety."

Amelia's breath caught. "Have you been raised from the dead?"

"Of course not!"

"Sister Manjra was ninety when she died, but she never came back."

"A body is only as old as they feel."

"How old do you feel?"

"Well, now that you've brought up the subject, I'm old as Methuselah. Now you best get those eggs cracked. Folks around here want their breakfast on time."

Amelia stuck the third piece of bacon in her mouth and slid off the counter to crack the remaining eggs as Izzy stirred the gravy. Methuselah! And the woman was still standing. Lord, bless her precious soul. She was a true fighter.

During breakfast, Amelia kept her eyes trained on Elizabeth, who sat beside Morgan, passing him biscuits and offering him gravy as if she owned him.

Izzy was kind enough to mention that Amelia had helped with breakfast. The rest of the crew commented on how nice that was of her, but Morgan remained silent. He buttered a fourth biscuit, doused it with honey, and ate it.

Amelia focused on the meat plate, and then her gaze drifted to the occupants of the long table. All of them except Morgan and the girls looked so old.

Izzy sat next to her husband, Enry, who spoke with an accent, perhaps French mixed with Irish. He was kind and always helpful when the women asked for anything. Next to Enry sat Niles, and then a roustabout, Ryder somebody. Amelia didn't know his last name. Everyone just called him Ryder. "Ryder, can you get me this?" "Ryder, can you get me that?" Ryder always did whatever was asked of him, but sometimes it took a while. He moved with a slow but determined sense of purpose. He sort of reminded Amelia of a doddering turtle. He moved with drawn-out precision, but he eventually got there.

When breakfast was over, Amelia helped Izzy and Enry clean off the long tables. Later she offered to dry while Izzy washed. "Enry is very nice. How long have you been married?" He was very nice, but Amelia couldn't look at anything but his big teeth. How did Izzy overlook them?

Izzy turned to look at her. "Who's Enry?"

"Enry. Your husband." Poor thing. Her mind *was* getting a bit feeble. And why not? Sister Agnes said of everything she'd lost, she missed her mind the most.

Izzy reached for a bowl. "I don't know Enry. Henry's my husband."

"Henry?" Her gaze flew to the man sitting beside Izzy. Enry.

Izzy shook her head. "Henry has a bit of an accent. Got a lot of Celtic in his blood. His ancestors came from Europe."

"Oh." Amelia's cheeks felt hot. Oh my goodness. She'd called the man Enry from the moment she'd boarded the boat. He must think her daft!

When she left the galley, the sun was full up, and the day promised to be nearly perfect weather. When she passed Elizabeth on the deck, she looked one way and Elizabeth looked the other.

Pilar was sitting on the bed in the first cabin, hands crossed, staring out a porthole when Amelia found her.

"Hi," Amelia said softly.

"Hi."

"Why are you sitting in here on such a lovely morning?"

"Thinking."

Amelia sat down to ponder with her. Izzy had said it would take well over a week to reach New Orleans. Other, newer vessels could go faster, but the *Mississippi Lady* was old and cantankerous sometimes. Crossing her hands, she studied the wall. It was going to be a long journey.

"It was nice of you to help Izzy with breakfast," Pilar offered.

"Do you know that she is ninety? Damp weather has her lumbago fired up again."

"Everybody's old around here. I wonder why?"

"Izzy said the crew has been together for years. They are more like family than employees. Seems Captain Jean Louis cares for each one and sees to their needs." Settling back on the bunk, Amelia recalled her earlier conversation with Izzy. "A long time

169

ago, Captain Matter used to captain a big passenger steamboat named the *Lucky Lady.* Izzy and Enry — do you know that Enry's name is actually Henry? Anyway, the captain and *Henry* worked together on that boat for a long time. A few years back, Captain Matter decided he was restless and didn't care to work so hard, so he stopped hauling passengers on the *Mississippi Lady* and started carrying cargo instead of people. Niles said he wanted to work for Jean Louis regardless. Well, Captain Matter said he didn't mind; in fact, he'd be right glad to have him.

"Now, Henry said he didn't want to work on the *Lucky Lady* without Niles. Jean Louis wanted Henry to move to the *Mississippi Lady,* because, like the rest of the crew, he was getting on in years and Jean Louis figured his crew was part of his family. Henry said he guessed he would move to the new boat if Captain Matter really wanted him. Captain said he wouldn't have said it if he didn't mean it.

"Then lo and behold, it turned out that Ryder, who had worked on the *Mississippi Lady* too, didn't have family, so he said if Henry was going to stay, he guessed he would too." Taking a deep breath, Amelia glanced at Pilar. "That's why everyone's so old."

Pilar stared back at her round-eyed. "Where did Izzy come in?"

"When she married Henry. The two had worked together for years, and she guessed she wasn't getting any younger, so when Henry proposed, she accepted. She told me it wasn't the way a man looked that made him special; it was his heart that made him exceptional."

"Where is Captain Jean Louis's wife?"

"He doesn't have one. Seems he and Morgan Kane have been longtime friends, and neither man has chosen to marry."

The two girls sat for a moment, each lost in thought.

"Where are the others?" Amelia asked.

Pilar frowned. "I don't know. After breakfast I came straight back to the cabin. I didn't want to get in anybody's way."

"Did you see how Elizabeth was making such a fuss over Morgan this morning at the breakfast table?" Amelia asked.

"Yes, but I don't think he's infatuated with her. I mean, not in a romantic way."

"Ha!"

Pilar sighed. "Men will be men," she said. "But he doesn't look at her the way he . . ."

"The way he what?"

"Looks at you."

"Me? He looks at me?"

"When you're not looking, as though he's trying to understand you."

"Ha. He thinks I'm a silly twit. And truthfully, I've behaved like one. I have not made the wisest decisions since we met. I am nothing but an annoyance to the man."

"Well, it seems to me that since you've had sort of a short acquaintance, you shouldn't judge one another. You barely know the man, but you're awfully critical of him at times."

"In the brief time we've been together, we have been through a lot, Pilar. When you're running for your life, you develop a mutual admiration simply trying to survive. Until I met the captain, I really didn't care for men. I know we fuss at each other, but the captain is a good man. I won't give him any trouble."

Pilar flashed a yearning smile. "Everybody's nerves are frayed." She sat in silence and then said, "I can't wait until I'm old enough to marry and have a real home."

"Your family?"

She shrugged. "They left me on an orphanage step when I was a week or two old."

Amelia reached to give her a hug. "We have a lot in common. A group of nuns took me and my two sisters in when we were very young." She smiled. "I understand the hunger you feel for a real home. I have two sisters, Abigail and Anne-Marie, so I have family, but I don't have a real home. A real home is special."

She often imagined a home with a mother and father. Mother would roast a big turkey on Christmas and make raisin pies. After they'd eaten, they would gather around a tall, freshly cut cedar trimmed in garlands the girls had made and sing songs. Then Pa would take the fiddle off the mantel and play "Amazing Grace," while Ma would work on hand-stitching a pillowcase before a blazing fire. Outside it would be snowing. Amelia's part of Texas didn't get snow, but she could dream, couldn't she? For those special nights, the world would be a small piece of heaven.

The nuns tried to provide festivities for the young sisters during the holidays, but most of their hours were spent in prayer, which was all right, since prayer was more important than parlor games. But every so often Amelia longed for just one game, a half hour of fun and laughter.

Getting up from the bunk, Amelia lifted her skirt, exposing her bare legs. "Tell me the truth. Is there anything wrong with my legs?"

Pilar seemed puzzled by the question.

"Your legs?"

"What's wrong with them?" Turning to the right and then to her left, Amelia waited for the verdict. "Too chubby?"

"No, nothing. They are nicely shaped. Not too plump but not too thin."

Sucking in a deep breath, Amelia thrust her chest forward. "What's wrong with these?"

Pilar's face flamed. "Amelia!"

"Yes. These." The sisters referred to the girls' endowments as "peach buds."

Pilar studied the body part. Finally, she shook her head. "Nothing. They look fine to me."

"They look fine to me too." Amelia hadn't considered her body often, but it appeared she was no different from other women her age. So why did Morgan find Elizabeth more appealing than her?

Pilar frowned. "Why are you worrying about your legs and . . . peaches?"

Turning to the side, Amelia sucked in her stomach. "It's my waist, isn't it? Too thick?"

"Not at all. You're practically skinny."

"It was smaller before I ate," Amelia admitted. Three pieces of bacon and three biscuits, she could admit, aggravated the situation.

Pilar nodded. "Mine too."

"My waist is smaller than Elizabeth's?"

Pilar thought for a moment. "I'd say they're about the same."

Releasing her breath in a whoosh, Amelia dropped back onto the bunk. "Then why does he prefer her?"

"He who?"

"Morgan. Why does he prefer Elizabeth? Why does he always hang around Elizabeth? Why does he always look at her?" She didn't know why his interest should worry her, but it did.

As Pilar pointed out, the two barely knew each other, and yet Amelia felt as though she'd known Morgan Kane a lifetime. She knew that he preferred wild game to beef. That he rose very early to watch the sunrise. That he believed in God and wasn't a drinking man, because if he was, he would have spent the past few days drunk. She knew his protective instincts often threatened his logical sense. He was a man of his word and a man of integrity. So much so, he would risk his job with the government to prevent eleven helpless women from being sold into slavery.

What was there not to like about Captain Morgan Kane?

"Maybe he doesn't prefer Elizabeth's company to yours. I don't see him paying much attention to her or any other woman. Maybe you're imagining his intentions."

"I didn't imagine it when he sent for Elizabeth on the clipper." She witnessed that plain as day. That wretched Austin Brown had come for Elizabeth and announced to the world that "Dov Lanigan" was in need of female companionship. Well, she might be naive, but she knew what that statement meant.

"You didn't imagine that, but maybe there were so many of us to choose from, Captain Kane decided to take potluck."

"Potluck, Pilar? Potluck!" Not only did Morgan not notice her, but she'd just been reduced to a picnic dish.

Pilar lowered her eyes. "Does it matter?" she asked softly. "Maybe Elizabeth didn't want to go. After all, she's as helpless in this matter as we are."

Sobering, Amelia pondered the observation. Was Morgan Kane the kind of man who would force himself on a woman? She could not imagine that he would. He had maintained a respectable distance with her, even when he could have easily taken advantage of her.

Amelia stood up, smoothing the wrinkles out of her dress. "I'm going fishing."

"Want me to come with you?"

"No, I need to think. I think best when I fish alone."

Days started to creep by. Captain Jean Louis had told Amelia stories about Morgan's childhood that made her laugh and wish she could have been there to see him. Before long, she began to feel as if she knew everything about Morgan Kane. Silas and Laura and Morgan's wonderful life growing up in an apple orchard. She felt she knew everything except his role in the war. Even Captain Jean Louis remained vague about his friend's occupation. It was important, Amelia was certain of that. A man like Morgan wouldn't do anything that wasn't worthwhile.

To her surprise, when she visited the wheelhouse one night, she saw Morgan sitting in the captain's seat. She turned in her tracks and started to leave when his voice stopped her.

"Looking for Jean Louis?"

"Yes. I thought I'd visit awhile." She'd taken to dropping by the wheelhouse after supper. Captain Jean Louis was a fascinating man with fascinating stories about whalers. He had read one report to her.

"Two points on the weather bow!"

"How far off?"

"A mile and a half!"

"Keep your eye on her!"

"Sing out when we head right!"

It turned out that three whales were descried from aloft in different parts, and in a short time, when we were deemed near enough, the captain gave orders to "Stand by and lower" for one a little more than half a mile to windward.

Three boats' crews pulled merrily away, glad of something to stir their blood, and with eager hope to obtain the oily material wherewith to fill their ship and make good their "lay." The whale was going leisurely to windward, blowing every now and again two or three times, then "turning tail," "up flukes," and sinking. The boats "headed" after him, keeping a distance of nearly one-quarter of a mile from each other, to scatter (as it is called) their chances.

Fortunately, as the oarsmen were "hove up," that is, had their oars a-peak, about the place where they expected the whale would next appear, the huge creature rose hard by the captain's boat, and all the harpooner in the bow had to do was to plunge his two keen cold irons, which are always secured to one towline, into the monster's blubber-sides. This he did so well as to hit the "fish's life" at once, and make him spout blood forthwith. It was the first notice the poor fellow had of the proximity of his powerful captors, and the sudden piercing of the barbed harpoons to his very vitals made him caper and run most furiously.

The boat spun after him with almost the swiftness of a top, now diving through the seas and tossing the spray, and then lying still while the whale sounded; anon in swift motion again when the game rose, for the space of an hour. During this time another boat "got fast" to him with its harpoons, and the captain's cruel lance had several times struck his vitals. He was killed, as whalemen call it, that is, mortally wounded, an hour before he went into "his flurry," and was really dead or turned up on his back.

The loose boat then came to the ship for a hawser to fasten round his flukes; which being done, the captain left his irons in the carcass and pulled for the ship, in order to beat to windward, and, after getting along-side, to "cut him in." This done, and the mammoth carcass secured to the ship by a chain round the bitts, they proceeded to reeve the huge blocks that are always made fast for the purpose to the fore and main mast head, and to fasten the cutting-in tackle. The captain and two mates then went over the sides on steps well secured, and having each a breast-rope to steady them and lean upon. The cooper then passed them the long-handled spades, which he was all the time grinding and whetting, and they fell lustily to work chopping off the blubber . . .

Soon after we had finished cutting in, about eight o'clock in the evening, the wind increased almost to a gale, making it impossible to try out that night. But today, while the ship is lying to, the business has begun in good earnest; the blubber-men cutting up in the blubberroom; others pitching it on deck; others forking it over to the side of the "try-works"; two men standing by a "horse" with a mincing knife to cleave the pieces into many parts for the more easy trying out, as the rind of a joint of pork is cut by the cook for roasting: the boatsteerers and one of the mates are pitching it into the kettles, feeding the fires with the scraps, and bailing the boiling fluid into copper tanks, from which it is the duty of another to dip into casks . . .

The whale now taken proves to be a cow whale, forty-five feet long and twenty-five round, and it will yield between seventy and eighty barrels of right whale oil. This is about the ordinary size of the New Zealand whale, a mere dwarf in comparison with that of the northwest, which sometimes yields, it is said, three hundred barrels, ordinarily one hundred and fifty, or one hundred and eighty.*

Sighing, Amelia said, "The captain has so many thrilling stories to tell."

"Yes, Jean Louis has lived a varied life," Morgan said. "I'm taking the wheel for a spell. The captain is having a second piece of pie with Izzy tonight."

"Oh my goodness." Amelia knew how the man would hate himself in the morning. "I told Izzy she shouldn't have baked pies today."

"You can visit with me," Morgan invited.

"Oh, no, thank you. I don't want to be a bother."

"Since when has that become a consideration?" He patted the seat beside him. "You want to pilot the boat for a while?"

"Pilot the boat?" Amelia was astounded. She couldn't think of a thing she'd like bet-

* Henry T. Cheever, *The Whale and His Captors* (New York: Harper and Brothers, 1853), chapter 3.

ter — except that he would pay more attention to her than Elizabeth.

Morgan scooted over, making room for her on the warped bench.

Amelia perched on the edge of the seat, feeling terribly self-conscious sitting so near to him. She detected the faint scent of soap and decided that he'd bathed at the rain barrel earlier.

"Here," he said, closing her hands over the wheel, "get a firm grip."

Before she realized what was happening, he'd slid behind her, his powerful arms bracing hers, his sure hands wrapped over her fingers, his firm chest supporting her back. He was so near that his breath tickled her ear. She could hardly breathe. She'd dreamed of being in his arms, but now that it was happening and so unexpectedly, she was stunned into silence.

Her knuckles turned white as she gripped the wheel tightly, trying to concentrate on steering the boat.

"Easy," he murmured, massaging her fingers. "Your hands will go numb. You don't have to take me so literally."

She tried to swallow the lump in her throat. "But the current," she whispered, her voice husky. "It's so strong. It keeps pulling at me. I can feel it through the wheel."

"Hold steady," he said next to her ear. "Don't fight it so much. Like this. You work with the pull, assessing how much resistance you need to apply." His fingers guided the pressure of hers against the wood. "Give and take. That's the secret. If you fight it like you were, you'll wear out in no time."

"Yes, that's better," she murmured. "There's so much I don't know."

There was a smile in his voice. "It's not so hard to learn when you want to."

She sighed. "I guess I'm a slow learner. I want to change, but old habits stick, and I forget to think." It was hard to concentrate when she was feeling his strength wrapped protectively around her, savoring the measured beat of his heart behind her shoulder.

"Keep your mind on what you're doing," he reminded.

I wish I could. How she wished she could confide in him her deepest longings and her greatest fears, and he would explain them.

She felt a bump, perhaps through her fingers on the wheel, or maybe through the soles of her shoes on the planked floor. "What was that?"

"Probably a sleeper," he said, scanning ahead.

"A submerged log?"

"I see you've been doing your homework."

"Henry told us about planters and sleepers the night we came aboard."

"Henry's spent his life on the river."

"It's a lovely river, but muddy."

"The muddy Mississippi — she's flowing fast with a lot of loose debris." He caught something out of the corner of his eye and turned to look back. Two Indians in a canoe were now following the boat.

Following his gaze over her shoulder, Amelia felt her heart spring to her throat when she saw the intruders. "What do they want?"

"Nothing, I suspect," he said calmly, glancing at them as he scanned the waters below. "Most likely they're intrigued by a 'fire canoe.' "

"Fire canoe?"

"That's what the red men call a paddle wheeler. Because of the sparks coming from the stack, they assume the boat is on fire." His attention focused on her. They were in such close proximity, she could feel the heat of his gaze on her skin.

"You don't really want to hear me tell you why the Mississippi is muddy, do you?" He skimmed a lock of stray hair from her cheek.

"Why don't you tell me what you've been up to?"

"Just normal things." She eased forward to the edge of the seat, his presence overpoweringly male.

"Where are you going?"

"Nowhere." She felt her cheeks growing red from his unnerving perusal.

They both fell silent for a moment as the boat plowed through the opaque waters. The Indians eventually turned away, paddling their canoe into an arm of the river.

His voice grew tender. "This has been quite an adventure. I'm sure you'll be glad when it's over."

"Yes — and no," she admitted with more vulnerability in her tone than she liked. Drawing her head to his shoulder, he held her for a moment.

"I'm sorry I've been so much trouble."

"I'm sorry I've been so cranky. Seems we both have been under a little strain lately."

"I've caused all the trouble, not you."

"Agreed," he teased softly.

She glanced to meet his eyes. "Oh, you." Nothing had been the same since she'd met him. Nothing ever would be again.

"Amelia, there's something you need to understand. If you have anything romantic in mind, my life is not my own — not yet."

He spoke as if he, too, had given thought to the future — maybe too much. They had known each other so briefly, and yet neither she nor he could deny that something enchanting happened when they were close. Their faces were now scarcely inches apart. She could see the tightening around his eyes, feel the intensity of his thoughts as he studied her. Instinctively, she leaned closer. The moment was more temptation than she could resist.

"I . . ." She couldn't mislead him. She'd done that too many times in the past. "Are you saying that you find me attractive?" She could hear her heartbeat in her throat.

"I didn't say that — not that I don't. You're a hard woman to overlook."

"Is this 'sweet talk'?" If so, she thought the words would be more gratifying. Romantic. There's was absolutely nothing satisfying about "You're a hard woman to overlook."

"I'm not saying that either . . ."

"The fact that we haven't known each other very long doesn't mean we can't feel . . . drawn to one another. Anne-Marie said sometimes people marry without even knowing the other. Arranged marriages. Have you heard of them?"

"Of course —"

"I wouldn't care for the arrangement. I'd want to choose my mate. Before I met you I really thought that I didn't care for men. Strange how that's changed." She glanced up. "Not that I'm in love with you. That couldn't be, not this fast, but the feelings I have give me hope that someday I'll meet a man like you and marry."

"Really."

"Really."

He drew back to look at her. "How did we get from muddy water to the subject of marriage?"

Now that the ice between them was broken, she might as well venture into the water. She'd never kissed a man, and Morgan Kane looked very kissable at the moment. Drawing his lips to hers, she kissed him in ways she hardly understood, letting new emotions guide her. She didn't care if her instincts ran astray. Had it not been for Jean Louis's unexpected return, the embrace might have gone on forever.

Instead, she broke away, scooting off the pilot seat. "Evening, Captain."

Jean Louis's gaze moved from Amelia to Morgan. A sly grin broke across his rugged features. "Hope I didn't interrupt anything important."

Morgan cleared his throat. "No. I was just

acquainting Amelia with the muddy Mississippi."

"Yes," the captain mused. "I sensed you
two were getting to know one another."

"The river is . . . extremely muddy."
Amelia gathered her skirt and smiled.
"Good evening, gentlemen."

Hastening to the door, she swallowed back
a lump of humiliation. What must Jean
Louis think of her now?

Amelia found Henry on the foredeck the
next morning. She sat down and visited for
a while until she inquired if he happened to
have any worms. He said that he did and
went to get them. When he returned, he was
carrying a large fruit jar full of dirt containing nice, fat river worms. After she talked
him out of one of his cane poles and the jar
of worms, she retired to the back of the boat.

Settling on a warped board, she stripped
off her shoes and wriggled her toes in the
water, relishing the sun's warmth.

She dug a worm from the jar, carefully
threaded it onto the hook, and cast her line
some twenty feet behind the boat. She
would have preferred that the boat was
moored, but since it wasn't, she'd have to
do the best she could. Curling her legs
under her torso, she prepared to do some

serious thinking. She had dared to kiss Morgan Kane. And he most definitely kissed her, but at her initiative. That didn't count. If he was truly attracted to her, he would have made the choice. She jerked and then landed her first perch. Pan size. She removed the hook, put on new bait, and then threw out again.

"Been fishing long?"

She recognized Morgan's voice, but her eyes remained on the bobber. "Long enough to catch one."

Leaning down, he extended a slice of something to her on the blade of the knife.

She eyed the offering suspiciously. "What's that?"

"Turnip. Eat it. It's good for you."

"I don't like turnips."

"Try a small bite. You're going to die of scurvy if you don't start eating fruits and vegetables."

"I'm not dead yet." Lifting the slice of turnip off the blade, she gingerly brought it to her lips.

He took a seat. "Eat it," he encouraged when her hesitation lingered. "It's not going to bite you."

Closing her eyes, she shoved the vegetable into her mouth, chewed quickly, and swallowed before she lost her nerve.

"That wasn't so bad, was it?"

It was neither bad nor good, but she'd stick with bacon. "How far to New Orleans?"

Morgan slipped a slice of turnip into his mouth. "Should arrive before week's end, maybe a few days afterward."

Today was Wednesday, which meant they were getting closer to their destination. The air seemed heavier with him around. It was an effort just to breathe deeply. She wished his presence didn't have such a staggering effect on her.

He shifted. "What are the others doing?"

"If you're referring to Elizabeth, I have no idea what she's doing." Her uncharitable tone left little doubt that she didn't care what Elizabeth was up to. The kiss she'd shared with Morgan wasn't easily forgettable. He had kissed back. Was Elizabeth the recipient of his stolen kisses, his stolen moments?

Tipping his hat over his eyes, he grinned and stretched out more fully on the deck. "I don't recall mentioning Elizabeth."

She kept her eyes on her line, wishing he would go away. She couldn't think straight when he was so near. She had deliberately sought privacy in order to think.

"Something just took your bait."

"Did not," she stammered when he caught her daydreaming. "That's the current."

"Something stole your bait," he repeated.

"Oh, for heaven's sake!" Just to show him, she pulled in her line and tried to ignore the smug look that lifted the corners of his mouth when she examined the stripped hook.

Grabbing the fruit jar, she dug for another worm. Every time she snagged one, it managed to wriggle out of her grasp. She could feel the heat of Morgan's gaze as she tussled with the enticement he caused within her. Her frustration mounted, and she attempted to redirect his attention. "Austin Brown must be pretty humiliated — and furious by now."

"I'd imagine he is."

She finally baited the hook and stood up to swing the line back into the water. It was useless to ignore Morgan. With an exasperated sigh, she sat down beside him. He wasn't the sort of man one could ignore for long.

Her brow bent into a frown. "Do you think he'll really try to follow us?"

"I know he will. Dov Lanigan has a great deal to lose if Austin Brown doesn't deliver."

She glanced over. She'd never thought much about how she looked, but the comments lately had seemed to imply that she was prettier than usual. She never considered herself to be anything but Amelia. "Do you think I'm pretty?"

He glanced over. "You're all right."

"Prettier than Elizabeth?" The question slipped out before she'd been aware of the thought. When he didn't answer, she thought he might not have heard her. When the silence grew increasingly awkward, she thought she would explode if he didn't answer the question. "Prettier than Elizabeth?" she repeated.

"What is this fascination you have with Elizabeth?"

Her tone had taken a personal turn. "I've seen the way she hovers around you."

He shrugged. "She's like a pup. Friendly."

"She's about as friendly as a sore bunion."

"Now, now," he chided. "What's Elizabeth done to you?"

She jerked her line, missing the catch. "Shoot." She reached for the bait jar.

"I am well aware that you and Elizabeth do not care for each other." Tipping his hat, he lay back to doze. "Why don't you leave each other alone, stop getting under each other's skin? Surely you can find something more productive to do than snarl at one another."

Snarl? He thought she snarled? What about Elizabeth and her cutting remarks? Had he taken note of them? Like her *snarling*? And for the record, she didn't snarl. She noted. There was a world of difference in snarling and noting. Anyone knew that.

Getting to her feet, she threw out her line and then sat down again. Suspicion gnawed at her nerves. "Has Elizabeth been talking about me?" She wouldn't put it past the woman. Criticizing her behind her back.

"Something got your bait again."

"Drat! At this rate, Henry will have to dig more worms when we reach the next landing."

She fell silent for as long as she could stand it. When her strained whisper broke the silence, her next question seemed to stun him. "Does she please you?"

He opened one eye. "What?"

"You favor her. Does she please you?"

He lifted his head and pinned her with a cold stare. "If you're asking what I think, you shouldn't be thinking or asking such things. I would have thought the mission nuns would have taught you better."

"I'm pretty sure they don't know *anything* about that sort of stuff."

"Nor should you."

"You act like I'm to blame for this conversation. *You* shouldn't be doing such things." She squared her shoulders defensively. "You're not married to her."

"To Elizabeth?" His tone rose.

"Look. I don't know what you *do* with Elizabeth. That's why I'm asking." Great balls of fire! Was the man dense?

He lay back again, adjusting his hat against the sun's unyielding rays. "That's right, you don't know what I do with anyone."

"Excuse me, but I thought that's been established. But God has given me eyes. I know that you and Elizabeth spend a lot of time together. I know what that means. I'm not a child." Shifting, she reverted to a safer subject. "What's in Washington Territory?" He'd said he was from there. Would he return once the war was over?

"Silas and Laura Stevenson are there."

"Jean Louis told me about your childhood. Laura and Silas are special people."

"The couple took me in when my mother couldn't keep me. Silas's health isn't good now, and he's no longer able to work his orchards. As soon as I'm finished here, I'm going back to help Laura."

"Orchards?"

"Apples. Silas raises the finest Jonathan apples you've ever put in your mouth."

"You don't have a father?"

A veil dropped over Morgan's features. "I'm sure I had a father, but I never knew him."

It would seem she was getting much too personal for his taste, and she was out of line with her questions. Jean Louis said Morgan's mother never returned to claim him. The subject was a touchy one, even though the small child had grown into a man. She handed him the pole. "I'm only here to think. I'll net what you catch."

He took the pole, examining the bait. "You can't think without a pole in your hand?"

"Not as hard. My sisters and I fished almost every afternoon if weather allowed. The nuns loved the fresh catch, and we hatched a lot of crazy plans during long summer days."

They sat in silence as Morgan threw out the line. A few pecks jiggled the bobber, but nothing took the bait.

"You going to be all right once we reach New Orleans?" he asked.

"Of course. I promise to book passage immediately for home." Unless he told her not to — which he wasn't going to do. He'd be only too glad to have her off his hands, though he had enough manners not to state the obvious.

"No dallying this time. I'm serious. You

have a tendency for drawing trouble."

"No dallying. Not one piddle, I promise."

"I believe we've had this conversation before."

"Yes, but I didn't mean what I said then. I do now." Smiling, she sighed. "I've been such a nuisance, and you have been very kind to me and the other women. I know I have delayed you from your work, and I apologize. If there's anything I can do to make up for —"

He grinned. "Just keep your promise and go home."

"Agreed."

Warm sunshine beamed from an unblemished sky. Right now the world was so peaceful and perfect, Amelia wished that time would stop. That the two of them could sit together all day until the sun slowly sank behind the water's edge.

"Your sisters must be concerned about you."

"When you happened along, I was truly blessed. I can only pray that the men who rescued my sisters are as honorable as you. Pure certainty strengthens my knowledge that God indeed shined on me the day you rescued me. If only Abigail and Anne-Marie were so blessed, though God has no reason to bless a single one of us.

"The McDougal hearts have always been in the right place, but youthful exuberance tainted our 'missions.' Our schemes have adequately kept the mission going for the past few years, but at what cost? The good ladies of the veil accepted our feebly concocted stories of strangers offering money for the old mission without question. Good-hearted people simply handing us coins when in truth, the three McDougals bilked innocent people. We knew what we were doing was wrong. Sinful. We once sold a herd of cattle that wasn't ours. A whole herd. The amount we gained from that little adventure kept the older nuns in food and necessities for a long time."

Morgan jerked and the line tightened. "Got one."

Amelia bent and netted a sizable sun perch. "Lovely!"

Morgan removed the catch and threaded a worm on the hook. "So you were actually Robin Hoods for the convent."

"We thought we were. Of course the nuns had no idea what we were doing. At first I didn't enjoy the ruse, but soon the excitement of our brazen exploits overrode my reservations. I suppose all three of us felt a rush of pleasure every time we successfully fooled someone and walked away unscathed. We especially enjoyed tricking men. Strange . . . but then, not so strange. Abigail detests men."

His brow lifted. "Abigail?"

"My sister." She shrugged. "I never thought to ask why, but she doesn't like men. She's pure tomboy. You would think she would take to men."

"She'll change when she meets the right man."

"Ha. There is no right man for Abigail."

"If I were a betting man, I'd wager there is. She'll run across him one day. She's still young."

He could be right. Amelia had thought she didn't like men. Until now. Her gaze strayed to the one sitting beside her. Lean, tanned. About as male and desirable as God ever made man.

He tossed the line back into the water. "How long did you ladies figure you could keep up that lifestyle?"

"Forever. We were very immature and misguided." She shifted. "I know I've learned my lesson. If Abigail and Anne-Marie survived, I have a hunch they'll be more than grateful to walk a straighter path."

He turned to focus on her. "Miss McDougal, I believe you mean that."

"I do. You can bank on it."

"So you plan to go back to Mercy Flats, to the orphanage, and remain there?"

"I do." Their gazes met and sobered. Before she knew what was happening, he lowered his head and kissed her. Not for a single moment did she pull away. In fact, she snuggled closer and settled in for the long-awaited embrace. When lips parted, she whispered, "Thank you, Morgan Kane."

"For what?"

"My first real kiss. I was beginning to think I'd never get one. This adventure has been so perfect, I would have hated for it to end with a handshake."

"I kissed you. The time —"

She placed her hand over his mouth. "But I started it. This one is most special."

His mouth lowered to take hers, long and sweet this time. Finally, he whispered, "I don't know what to do about you, Amelia McDougal."

"I know, but I have every confidence you'll think of something, Captain Kane." She lowered his head for another kiss. They could talk later.

Eight

Amelia presented the perch to Izzy, who promised to bake the catch for supper. Amelia felt a pang of disappointment. The convent nuns coated fish in cornmeal and fried the pieces in a deep iron skillet with simmering bacon grease, whereas Izzy simply doused the fillets with flour and baked them. Mahalia had fried fish one night, and they had been delicious.

Early that evening Amelia gathered the women on deck. If the men aboard thought anything was amiss, they went about their work with occupied expressions.

Elizabeth let it be known that she was attending the hastily called assembly to satisfy her curiosity, nothing more. The other women wore curious expressions.

"I think Izzy, Niles, Henry, and Ryder are too old to be waiting on us," Amelia began. "I know this is a late thought, but for the remainder of the journey, we need to take over the cooking and cleaning duties."

Bunny frowned. "The men's duties?"

"Not all of the men's jobs. We know nothing about sailing a vessel, but we can help Izzy and Henry."

"I can clean," Pilar offered. "I've always been good at cleaning."

"And I can sew," Faith said. "I'm good at crocheting and knitting, things like that."

Amelia nodded, relieved that they were taking to the idea. The elderly should be respected, and Izzy and Henry had passed elderly and were headed for ancient. "I don't know if there's a need for crocheting or knitting, but we can ask."

"I can cook," Mahalia offered hesitantly. "I can make fine hotcakes, light as thistle-down, and there is no reason one of us can't keep the boiler stoked."

"The boiler, of course. I've tasted your fish and it's delicious. And hotcakes. That's the spirit!"

"I'll do the wash," Bunny said. "I always did the family wash before I was captured."

"Thank you, Bunny. Izzy will be ever so grateful."

The women had seen to their own needs, but the men didn't appear to lift a finger when it came to washing and cooking. Extra hands would be welcome.

Following the meeting, the women, with Amelia in the lead, marched to the wheelhouse to tell Captain Jean Louis of their plans. Elizabeth remained behind.

"Assume Izzy's workload? That's mighty gracious of you, ladies." Drawing on his pipe, he nodded approval. "She'll be pleased as a peacock."

"Invade my galley?" Izzy sank to the nearest stool when Amelia told her their plan. The older woman wiped sweat from her brow with the hem of her apron. "How soon can you start?"

Amelia brightened. "You don't mind?"

"Mind? Mercy, no! The sooner the better."

Henry, Niles, and Ryder reacted the same. Showing a mouthful of horse teeth, Henry said, "Girls, you're a blessing sent from above! The boiler needs wood."

"Sorry we didn't think of it earlier," Amelia apologized. "But you'll have a few days of doing nothing but what you choose."

Faith approached Henry with a shy smile and a gentle voice. "I'd be glad to take care of the boiler, Henry. I can also sew real nice, and tonight I'll keep the boiler stoked so you can enjoy an uninterrupted night of sleep."

Henry's smile broadened, and Amelia tried not to stare. He was such a good man. He couldn't help that he had big teeth. "That's kind of you, girl." Henry hurried off to return with the most awful pile of sewing Amelia had ever seen. Izzy must not own a needle.

Roles reversed. Mahalia assumed Izzy's role in the galley. Faith repaired tears and sewed buttons on clothing while the others scrubbed the old vessel clean except for the crew quarters, which, after one look, Amelia declared hopeless and shut the door. Everyone aboard appeared happy with the new arrangements — except Elizabeth, who, it seemed, wouldn't have been pleased if the good Lord had offered to appoint her His left hand.

The Mississippi rolled peacefully along as the old boat slowly carried its unusual cargo to New Orleans. At times Amelia wondered if Austin Brown and his men were somewhere lurking around the next corner, but she was so busy with her new duties, she didn't have the time to give the dreadful idea more than a fleeting consideration.

For the second time, she and Morgan fished from the back of the boat in the late afternoon. It was, Amelia told the Lord most humbly, another one of the best days of her life.

Before dropping off to sleep that night, she sat straight up from her bed nestled between two bunks with an even fresher idea. Outside a thunderstorm raged, rocking the old paddle wheeler like a fussy infant. Why not make the boat more . . . homey? The worn curtains were dirty and ugly, and the storm would delay them another day. Already she'd felt the boat anchor sometime after ten o'clock as gusty winds pitched the boat. That meant they had at least two more days before they reached their destination. Much could be accomplished in that time. New curtains. Fresh new hangings in the sleeping quarters. With every woman involved, the task could be accomplished in a matter of hours. Amelia reached over and shook Pilar awake and whispered her plan.

Tonight's roommates, Ria, Mahalia, Pilar, and Hester, immediately took to the idea. Elizabeth lay nearby, wearing a disagreeable frown.

"We'll start first thing in the morning," Pilar said. "We can have new hangings completed by the time we reach New Orleans."

Amelia nodded. "A simple cotton print

that could be taken down and washed would do a lot to brighten up the old boat. Lace trim around the hems would make a nice finishing touch. Nothing fancy, just something to make the curtains even prettier. Izzy deserves a few feminine touches around here."

Mahalia agreed. "We don't have the funds for new material, but we could remake the old hangings. The trim could be our contribution to the boat, a little something of ourselves that will remain long after we're gone. I have five cents I can contribute."

"I love to work with any kind of material," Faith exclaimed. "Sewing is my special talent. I've never been good at cooking or homemaking, but when it comes to sewing, I'm more than capable."

"I have money." Amelia shook her head. "How blind I was — but my eyes are fully opened now. Never again will I be prey to a man like Brown. My eyes have been opened to the world's true evil. My sister Abigail would be completely right to mistrust and despise a man with a serpent's tongue, but all men are not like Brown, thank You, God. Morgan, Jean Louis, Henry, Niles, Ryder — they are good men with good hearts. A woman should be proud to claim any one of these men as hers."

Sleepy agreements mixed with a clap of thunder.

As the *Mississippi Lady* rocked back and forth in the storm, the women set their sights on a few yards of lace. The problem would be getting the men to stop long enough to make the purchase.

"Until we reach New Orleans, the captain isn't likely to stop for any reason except to take on wood. First town we come to, I'll slip away and buy the lace," Amelia decided. Her earlier promise to Morgan to obey struck her. "No. I can't. I promised I would do as Morgan says, and that is to stay put."

Pilar's expression turned thoughtful. "As nice as curtains would be, I think every one of us should cause the least trouble we can. Both captains are doing their best to save us from harm."

"And the next stop might not be a town," Mahalia said.

Once their boat stopped midriver to buy wood from a farmer who'd piled it along the banks. And the women knew without being told that Captain Jean Louis and Morgan would both think it far too hazardous to voluntarily stop to buy something as frivolous as lace. Austin Brown was likely not far behind by now, and neither captain would consider taking unnecessary risks with the women's safety.

"Perhaps Captain Jean Louis can be persuaded to make a brief stop," Faith reasoned. "It wouldn't take long to buy a few yards of lace."

"The windows are fine the way they are." Elizabeth rolled to her side and pulled a blanket over her head. "The men will spit nails if you put curtains up on this boat."

"Both captains have taken unnecessary risks to help, so it only seems right that we do something to repay them," Auria ventured.

"I agree," Bunny spoke up. "I don't have any one special talent, but I would like to do something to show my gratitude. We could be on our way to New Orleans as purchased women."

"Then we are of like mind." Amelia shot Elizabeth's covered head a you'd-better-not-throw-a-kink-in-the-plan look. "If Faith wants to put lace on the curtains, she can. Okay, Elizabeth?"

Elizabeth clutched the pillow tighter.

"Maybe we can speak to Jean Louis alone. Surely one small stop isn't so frivolous," Faith reasoned. "If the captain says no, then the matter is settled. We do as the men say."

"Now the big question. Who will ask for permission to buy the lace?" Auria asked.

"I'll ask him." Amelia didn't mind. A simple question wouldn't break her promise to Morgan to stay out of trouble. If lacey curtains helped to repay Jean Louis for his kindness, then she was happy to be their appointed spokeswoman.

When Amelia told him the plan, Captain Jean Louis didn't like the idea any better than Elizabeth did. "I don't think that's wise," he said. "Besides, we have enough wood to reach our destination. The added weight would only slow us down."

"Buying lace wouldn't take long," she reasoned, "and it would make Faith feel good. Each of us would like to repay you for your help."

"You ladies are not expected to contribute anything," the captain said. "Prayers are the exception. This little escapade is far from over, Miss McDougal . . ." A grin began to spread slowly across his features. "Have you mentioned the curtains to Morgan?"

Amelia sighed as she glanced to the port side, peering back between the paddles of the big wheel. "I haven't said anything to him yet."

"Lacey curtains." The captain's grin widened, and Amelia was tempted to think Jean Louis found the request humorous.

"On second thought, it wouldn't hurt to take on wood. Wouldn't want to run low, not when we're so near our destination. We'll make a brief stop early in the morning, and one of you can purchase the lace as long as you do so quickly. If you dally, I'm afraid I will have to leave without you. Is that understood?"

"Yes, sir! And thank you! The girls will be so pleased." She was tempted to give him a hug but changed her mind. The action would be entirely too personal. "I'll tell the others."

"Amelia?"

She turned. "Yes?"

"Don't mention the lace to Morgan. He's a bit stuffy about staying on track. We'll keep this a secret between us."

"I understand. I won't say a word."

"Good." He fished in his pocket. "Let me contribute to the gesture." He removed a bill from his wallet and handed her the money. "Buy something bright and sunny. I'm looking forward to seeing my good friend's face when you present the surprise." His grin turned to pure scalawag.

Amelia noticed the change and wondered what the captain found so amusing about a bit of lace, but at least he was on board with the plan. That's all she cared about.

■ ■ ■ ■

Amelia had been designated to distract Morgan while Pilar purchased the lace. The paddle wheeler docked shortly after breakfast to take on wood, and the women flew into action. Not fifteen minutes later, Morgan led Amelia inside the small galley, motioning for her to sit down.

"What's wrong?" Izzy glanced up from the rocker she was sitting in. The boat's old tomcat was curled around her feet, purring loudly. Mahalia bustled around the small galley storing breakfast pots.

"Miss McDougal seems to be in dire need of something constructive to occupy her time today."

Amelia glared. "I thought of something worthwhile to occupy my time."

"Teaching the women to play poker is hardly constructive, Amelia."

She shrugged. "They wanted to learn." She could tell him that it was her job to distract him, and she knew the ploy would certainly catch his attention.

"I think your time is better spent with Izzy this morning."

"But that's Mahalia's job —"

"Sit."

"Where's Mahalia?" Amelia winced when Mahalia suddenly appeared in the galley doorway with a heaping pan of potatoes and set them in her lap. Outside the porthole, sounds of men loading wood aboard the paddle wheeler drifted to her. Her stomach fluttered with anxiety. She had prayed long and hard that the simple purchase would take place without incident. Pilar drew the short straw, so she would make the purchase. She wouldn't do anything to risk anyone's safety.

Amelia reached for a paring knife. "How many do I have to peel?"

Mahalia grinned. "Every last one of them."

While Amelia distracted Morgan, Pilar had left the boat for a few minutes to buy lace. Amelia's insides squirmed with apprehension as she focused on the long spirals of potato peels curling around the knife and dangling in front of the dozing cat's nose.

Chicken simmered on the stove, bread was baking in the oven, and it appeared that Izzy had dozed off in her chair. Mahalia glanced up. "You really wantin' something else to do?"

Amelia sighed again. "I need something to take my mind off of Pilar." The girl was most dependable, but if any small distraction slowed her return, the boat would leave without her. One thing Amelia had learned about Jean Louis — the man kept his word.

Izzy stirred and opened her eyes. "Can't think of a thing. Mahalia has meat simmering. Bread baking. I don't know what to do with my hands now that you girls are in charge of the galley." Blinking sleep out of her eyes, the old woman said, "Instead of keeping me company, why don't you go up and see if you can't carry on a conversation with Morgan without sparks flying?"

"No, thank you, Izzy. He just dumped me here to get me out of his hair."

Izzy chuckled. "And a mighty attractive head of hair it is. Seems like you're missing a good chance to catch the captain's eye. Seems a nice man like Morgan might need a little female nudge, if you know what I mean."

"I know what you mean, but as much as I wish it were true, I don't feel he returns my affection. Not really."

"Well." Izzy grunted and pushed to her feet. "All I know is he'd be a fine catch for someone. Jean Louis says the young captain needs a wife to settle him down."

"I would welcome the opportunity, but Morgan falling deeply in love with me won't happen." Even voicing the thought gave her shivers.

Izzy washed the potatoes, poured fresh water in the pan, and set them on the stove to boil. Mahalia shooed her off with a dish towel. "Git! Git out of my way, girl. Get some fresh air. Take a nap. Spend some time with Henry. I'm in charge for the time being."

"Mahalia?" Amelia glanced around the galley, looking for the usual pies cooling on the shelf. None were present this morning. "Didn't you make pies earlier?"

Izzy spoke up. "Told her not to. Jean Louis is still complaining that he's gaining weight like a prize hog." She reached into the wood box and got a few more sticks to throw into the stove. Mahalia flipped the towel in her direction. "Git."

Amelia sighed. "No dessert?"

"Not today." Izzy straightened, clutching the small of her back. She glared at Mahalia.

"I'm going!" Shortly after, the galley screen door slapped shut.

Sliding off the counter, Amelia moseyed around, peering into cabinets and cubbyholes. A frown formed around the corners of Mahalia's mouth. "Looking for something?"

"No." Amelia opened a jar of peaches and

213

ate a piece. "Is it hard to bake a cake?"

"Nothing hard about it. You never baked a cake?"

"Just thinking out loud." She dug out another peach half, tilted her head back, and let the juice drizzle down her throat. She was trying her best to tolerate these things.

"Didn't you get enough to eat at breakfast?"

Amelia glanced up. "Plenty. Why?"

"Just wondering."

Moving to the oven, Amelia checked on the loaves of baking bread. She fumbled for two large hot pads and then removed six crisp loaves from the oven and set them out to cool. The bread smelled so good, she pinched off a bite of the thick brown crust and popped it into her mouth. It was so tasty, she pinched off another bite and chewed it thoughtfully.

"Mahalia, is it really true that the way to a man's heart is through his stomach?"

"How would I know? Never known a man." Sorrow filled her eyes when the young black girl met her gaze. Elizabeth's earlier taunts about Mahalia came back to haunt Amelia. *Ask her. She tried to escape, and they caught her. Ask her what they did.*

"Oh, I am so sorry, Mahalia."

The young girl with soft brown eyes straightened. "If you don't mind, I think I'll go to the rain barrel and wash up. Can you keep an eye on the chicken?"

"I'd be happy to. Take all the time you need."

Mahalia left, and Amelia turned to study the small work area. Cooking seemed an odd way to deepen Morgan's attraction — if there was one. Since she couldn't hold a candle to Elizabeth in the worldly department, perhaps a nice, tasty sweet would be an effective weapon.

She searched the pantry for something to create that would be so irresistible, even Morgan would be impressed. Apple pie would be the first choice, since he seemed to be partial to apples, but there were no apples. She settled for a cake.

Morgan no doubt thought that she was so young and foolish that she wouldn't know how to do the simplest things. Well, she'd show him. She'd bake a cake that he'd never forget.

Tying on an apron, she begin to rummage in the pantry and took out flour, sugar, a pinch of salt, three large dollops of lard, and so on. The convent sisters preferred natural fare, and sweets were rarely kept in the kitchen. On special occasions, Sister

Lucille made popcorn balls during the months they gathered honey from the two hives they kept far from the convent.

Sister Camille's cooking advice floated through her head. "I never measure — I dump. Eventually you get the hang of it."

Tying an apron around her waist, Amelia set to work. Selecting a large wooden bowl, she dumped ample amounts of flour and sugar from two of the largest jars. She wanted a large cake, enough to feed the crew, so she dumped in another cup of flour and sugar for good measure.

Dipping into the lard bucket, she doled out a hefty chunk and then added salt and baking soda.

Selecting five eggs, she cracked them one by one into the bowl. Peering at the concoction, she decided that the batter didn't look right, so she added three more. Now it looked like there were more eggs than flour and sugar, so she added another cup of sugar. Then there was more sugar than eggs and lard, so she added another hefty cup of flour.

She glanced up when she felt a slight jarring motion, as though the crew was making a repair to the vessel.

Turning back, she studied the cake mixture and then snapped her fingers. Searching through the pantry, she located a jar of applesauce and seasoned the batter with a generous splash.

Reaching for a wooden spoon, she tried to stir the gooey mixture, but it just knotted up into greasy, odd-colored hunks.

She stepped to the water bucket for liquid. By now, the mixture was nearly overflowing the bowl.

Blending the concoction until it was frothy, she realized she was going to have a huge cake on her hands. But that was good. There were a lot of people on hand to enjoy it.

She dropped to her hands and knees and rummaged through the pantry for a pan big enough to hold the concoction. She settled on a roaster, the only thing large enough to hold the batter.

Her eyes measured her creation. Something didn't look right. The batter looked nothing like she'd seen at the mission. She sighed. Cooking was not going to be her long suit. Should she dump the mess and start over? Her practical side overrode common sense. The fixings were all edible, ordinary ingredients. The cake might be overly large, but it would surely be edible.

Greasing the roaster with another hunk of lard, she liberally sprinkled more flour into the bottom and shook it around until the pan was lightly coated.

Pouring the batter carefully into the pan, she then picked it up and moved gingerly to the stove. Setting the cake down on the stovetop, she opened the oven door and studied the small area. It didn't look wide enough to hold the roaster.

Removing the baking hens, she set the meat out to cool. After a few unsuccessful tries, she managed to wedge the roaster into the oven and close the door. She had no idea how long it would take to bake this size of a cake, but she supposed instinct would tell her when it was done. Undoubtedly, it would take a good deal of baking time.

After returning to the sink, she washed her hands, dried them, and then hurried in search of Pilar. The boat would be leaving any moment. When she stepped outside, the crew were taking on wood, talking among themselves as they worked. In the distance, a man's voice lifted in anger.

Voices ballooned into a shouting match between two dockworkers. From what Amelia could gather, the two men were arguing over a woman.

A shot rang out. Amelia's hands flew up to cover her ears as she looked toward the landing. A man lay on his back, a crimson stain spreading across the front of his shirt.

Horrified, she froze in place, unable to believe what she witnessed. Ripping her apron off, she flew to the side of the boat, eager to see the action.

Morgan walked by the galley and noticed black smoke rolling from a pan of potatoes on the stove that had boiled dry. Entering the galley, he grabbed for the hot pads, dragged the pot off the stove, and flung it into the sink.

When the smoke cleared, his eyes focused on the oven where a strong smell caught his attention. Stepping closer, he opened the oven door. His eyes quizzically searched the roasting pan. Leaning closer, he sniffed, trying to identify the aroma. When he failed, he lifted one end of the pan, surprised at its weight. Obviously it was something Izzy or Mahalia was attempting to bake, but he couldn't identify the object.

Whatever it was, the thing stunk.

There was nothing like a shooting to liven things. Amelia stood on one foot and then the other, trying to see above the crowd.

The injured man on the ground was rolling around, carrying on something awful as a man bent over him.

Amelia spotted Henry and ran to join him. "What happened?"

"Female troubles," Henry told her with a toothy grin.

"They're fighting over a woman?" Amelia stood on her toes, straining to see the conflict. She'd never seen anyone fight over a woman before.

"Yep, they sure are." Henry gave her another overhanging grin. "Fightin' over one of them showboat gals."

"A showboat?" Amelia's eyes pivoted to scan the landing. "There's a showboat here? I've never seen a showboat," she said softly. "Ever." Of course Abigail knew all about them. She said women danced and sang wearing skimpy dresses while men gambled and drank strong whiskey into the wee hours of morning.

"Right there, big as you please." Henry pointed to the landing where the magnificent, gaily lit spectacle was moored.

"A showboat," Amelia murmured in awe. "An honest-to-goodness showboat." The boat was a sight to behold. Grabbing Henry's hand, she pulled him down the gangplank and toward the big, glossy white paddle wheeler. Gilded lettering glinted in the afternoon sun. Intricate molding outlined the doorways. It was the most splendid sight she'd ever seen!

"Now hold on, girl. We've got to get back to the *Mississippi Lady* before she leaves without us," Henry warned. He glanced over his shoulder.

"She can't leave without us." Amelia pointed to the boats congregated around the landing. The shooting had caused so much attention, the ruckus momentarily paralyzed river traffic.

"Captain's not gonna like this," Henry said. His short legs pumped to keep up.

"I only want to see the boat up close." Amelia pulled him along firmly. "Have you heard they have painted women and really immoral men on these things?"

"Yes, ma'am," Henry panted. "I've heard that."

"Hurry, Henry. Hurry!"

"Yes, ma'am. I'm hurrying." His bandy legs pumped faster.

The only force strong enough to repel Amelia at that moment was the solid wall she suddenly slammed into.

Bouncing a foot backward, her foot caught in the hem of her dress, and she toppled over, feeling momentarily dazed as her head reeled and she saw stars. The wall she'd run into spoke in a booming voice that sent her blood to pumping. "Who did you *shoot*?"

Peering groggily up at the voice, Amelia's shoulders relaxed when she saw Morgan. "What?"

"Why are you off the boat!"

"Because it isn't going anywhere for a while!" Climbing back to her feet, she confronted the captain crossly. "What are *you* doing off the boat?"

His eyes swung to her wheezing accomplice. "Henry, what is going on here?"

"Well, sir, first I said . . . and then she said . . . and of course then I warned her —"

"Henry didn't do anything." Amelia brushed dirt off of her hands and knees. "We were just going to see the showboat."

"You were told to stay aboard the *Mississippi Lady*."

"I *was* staying aboard until I heard gunshots! Everyone else went to look, so I did too."

"Haven't you been told explicitly not to leave the boat?" Their eyes locked in mute combat.

After a staring contest, Amelia broke eye contact first when she glanced away and shrugged. "I didn't intend to be gone long."

Henry finally caught his breath. "If you two don't mind, I'll just be going on back to the boat." He turned and left before Amelia could object.

"What's this about a shooting?" Morgan turned and fell quickly into step behind Henry.

"Where have you been? There was one right over there." Amelia pointed to the crowd that was still gathered around the fallen man. "Two men were fighting over a woman, and one shot the other."

Morgan paused, removed his hat and knocked the dust from it, and settled it back on his head wearily. "I've been cleaning the lower part of the paddle wheel. I didn't hear the ruckus until the noise grew so loud I came to investigate."

"Morgan." She stooped, winded. "Couldn't we just see the showboat? The *Mississippi Lady* can't possibly move for at least a half hour."

He frowned. "It's a gambling boat."

"I won't go aboard. I'll take one peek." Grabbing his hand, she pulled him in the opposite direction. She had never seen a showboat up close, and she might never have the chance to see one again. Oh, the stories she'd have to tell Abigail and Anne-Marie! A real, honest-to-goodness, sin-ridden, immoral showboat, and she had stood in front of it.

"It's splendid." She stood at the bank admiring the floating palace. The boat gleamed with a fresh coat of paint, and with its brightly colored flags snapping in the breeze, the vessel had an air of celebration about it. "Isn't it splendid?" she breathed. "Have you ever been aboard one?"

"Yes, once or twice."

Amelia knew no lady should be seen stepping aboard a showboat, but oh, how she'd love to slip inside those grand rooms for a glimpse of that other life.

Morgan shook his head, but a smile escaped. "It's not so grand."

"Men are lucky." Sighing, Amelia sat down on the ground, her eyes never straying from the showboat. "I've never done anything exciting like that. What's it like to be aboard one?"

"What's it like? Well, for days, prior to their arrival, colorful posters are pinned to trees, fences, barns, and outbuildings. People shout, 'Showboat a-comin' up and down the river when the spectacle pulls into port. A loud calliope plays a jaunty melody as the floating theater arrives in small river towns, usually early morning.

"The larger showboats often have a brass band that will make a big production of parading through the center of a community, attracting a crowd. Actors, crew, everybody aboard traipses about, enticing audiences to the evening performance.

"That night the path to the showboat is marked by the fiery splendor of oil flares mounted on poles.

"Once aboard, the audience is entertained by an orchestra until the curtain rises. From early spring until late autumn, the local residents are charmed by plays, vaudeville, and circus acts."

Clasping her hands together tightly, she gazed at him, her cheeks warm with excitement. "Did you see a show?"

He chuckled. "My first visit, the actors put on a play about a sickly looking heroine who wandered from town to town, looking for a cure for her illness. The villain tried to deceive her by keeping her away from the cure. In the end the hero arrived in the nick of time to save her."

Amelia grinned. "Exactly how did he save her?"

"With a magical remedy for her illness. When he gave her a spoonful of potion, she was immediately healed. The villain was foiled, and the heroine returned to full, glowing health. Then the curtain closed, and the captain stepped out carrying a bottle of the magic elixir. 'Ladies and gentlemen,' he proclaimed" — Morgan spread his arms with a grand flourish — " 'the miraculous medicine that has cured our lovely heroine can do the same for you!' "

"And people purchased bottle after bottle?" Her eyes glowed with excitement, trying to imagine it all.

"Fifty cents. Three for a dollar!" he mocked.

"Was the potion really magical?"

"No," he scoffed. "Many were taken in by the captain's promises for robust health, but alas, the magic elixir was nothing more than river water with color added after the mud had been drained off."

"Oh, but it still must have been wondrously exciting," she said. "To see all those people and hear the music. Did you ever see a real play?"

"Yes, a few."

"What? What did you see?"

"I saw *Bertha the Sewing Machine Girl*."

"Oh! That must have been fun. *Bertha the Sewing Machine Girl*. What wonderful adventures you've had!"

"Actually, it was a melodrama that had all the women in the audience sobbing before it was over."

"You've only seen one?"

"No, there was *Ten Knights in a Bar Room,*

and *East Lynne.*"

"Oh, the life you've led. I envy you so much," she whispered. Her eyes returned to the colorful showboat. "Does it cost much to see one of these plays?"

"I think the usual charge is fifty cents."

"Fifty cents. That's a lot."

"Not so much." His eyes gentled when he gazed at her. "Maybe somebody will take you to see a play someday."

"I don't think so. I understand that no lady should be seen going aboard a showboat."

"Well," he said softly, "perhaps if the lady is in the company of a reputable gentleman, it wouldn't be improper."

Amelia longed for the day when a woman could do the same things a man could. It hardly seemed right that the males got to have all the fun.

"We need to go," Morgan urged gently. "Jean Louis will be leaving shortly."

Sighing, Amelia lifted her hand, and he helped her to her feet. They fell into step, heading for the paddle wheeler.

"It's sad that there's so much good in the world that can't be enjoyed because of the evil," she said.

"For instance?"

"Well, if it weren't for Austin Brown, the

evil, then we could stay for a while, and you could take me to one of the showboat performances. That would be good. Maybe, somehow, we could all go. Even Elizabeth," she added, feeling generous.

Morgan chuckled. "You would be willing to include 'ol' rotten' Elizabeth?"

Amelia refused to look at him now. "Only because I know you would want her along."

"I'm not sure I would take you, even if I could. Over the years, the respectability of a showboat has diminished, and many arrivals have been met by groups of armed citizens inviting the theater to keep moving."

"Still," she murmured, "it's sad that there are people like Dov Lanigan and Austin Brown in this world."

They walked in silence a stretch before Morgan spoke again. "How is Austin Brown any different from you and your sisters?" His observation was made without malice, but it had no less impact.

"What?"

"How is what Austin Brown and his men do any different from what you and your sisters do?"

"I admit that my sisters and I were misguided youth. Austin Brown is pure evil," she said. "My sisters and I meant no harm.

We never hurt anyone. Everybody we took from could afford the loss."

"You were stealing."

"No, it wasn't really stealing," she argued. "And everything we took was for the mission."

"Sin has no assigned color," Morgan theorized.

His words stung, but they were true. Sin was black, little or large.

"Do you think I'm evil?"

His features sobered. "Amelia, a person is judged by his integrity. The word means that a man — or a woman — doesn't cheat or steal or lie to gain what he or she wants."

"Then how does she get what she wants if she doesn't have the funds to pay for it?"

His look was direct and candid. "She comes by it honestly, or she does without."

Neither spoke for a moment while Amelia tried to absorb the full meaning of his words.

"How do you know so much about integrity?" she finally asked.

"Laura, the woman who raised me, taught me about it."

"Laura must be very wise." The sisters had taught her many things, and undoubtedly they tried to teach her integrity, but somehow it must not have stuck.

"She's a good woman."

"Were the two of you close?"

"Very close. Laura took in washing and ironing to make ends meet." He smiled. "She used to tell me that we were so poor, the church mice looked prosperous."

"Your mother never returned for you?"

"No." His features closed. "In a way, you remind me of Laura."

Amelia paused, turning to look at him. "I look like her?" That must mean that he thought she was good too. Her heart nearly burst with happiness.

"No, you look nothing like Laura," he admitted. "But she is a strong woman."

"Strong?" Amelia wasn't sure she wanted him to think of her as a manly brute.

Up ahead they spotted a gypsy selling wares from her cart.

"A lovely flower for your lady?" The gypsy extended a single daisy for Morgan's inspection.

Pausing, Morgan examined the flower. "Very pretty."

"Only a pittance, sir," the gypsy tempted. Her faded brown eyes rested on Amelia. "Small price for one so comely."

"You're right, it is a small price." Reaching into his pocket, he extracted a coin. "Would you have any tobacco?"

"Aah." The old woman's smile wreathed her whole face. "That I do. How much would you like?"

"Two sacks will do, thank you."

She handed him the two small pouches, and he paid her.

Amelia watched the exchange with a sinking heart. The tobacco, she felt sure, was a gift for Elizabeth.

"And two apples," he added.

"Excellent choice, kind sir." Smiling, the gypsy woman polished the fat, round apples before handing them to him.

Turning, Morgan presented the daisy and one apple to Amelia. "For the lovely lady."

"Thank you." Lifting the daisy to her nose, Amelia twirled it between her fingers, letting the petals softly brush her skin.

"Read your fortune, sir?" the gypsy tempted.

"No, thank you." He paid the gypsy for the apples.

As they approached the *Mississippi Lady,* Amelia could see Captain Jean Louis in the pilothouse, motioning for the couple to come aboard. The crowd at the dock was dispersing, and river traffic was moving again. Pilar stood at the railing, holding a small parcel.

Crossing the gangplank, Morgan pulled

Amelia protectively to the railing as Henry lifted the crossing and the boat slowly swung upstream.

"Morgan," Amelia whispered, enjoying the brief feel of his arms around her. "Thank you for taking me to see the showboat." The past few minutes with him had been a tiny piece of heaven.

Gazing down at her, he smiled. "It was my pleasure."

Her heart must be in her eyes now. "Do you honestly think I'm evil?"

Squeezing her waist, he refused to meet her gaze, but his tone didn't sound judgmental. "Misguided, perhaps. But very pretty."

She didn't want to believe that she and her sisters could be as bad as Austin Brown and his thugs.

A warm rush of hope spread through her. On impulse, she rose on her toes and kissed him lightly on the lips.

His eyes reflected a difference she had never seen before. Taking her by the waist, he moved her into the deep dimness of the stairway.

Their eyes met briefly before he lowered his mouth to hers, kissing her gently but very thoroughly. Only the sound of Mahalia's screech broke the silence. *"What is that thing in the oven?"*

NINE

The *Mississippi Lady* resumed her journey. Supper was late that evening, but nobody minded. The day had been exciting to say the least. The cake was a dismal failure, but Amelia took the ribbing good-naturedly.

"Next time," Izzy said, "ask for help. Waste of flour and sugar."

Amelia crossed her heart. "You have my solemn word."

For some nameless reason, Izzy, Jean Louis, Niles, and the others had become her family — all but Morgan. Her gaze had touched on the man who now held the key to so many emotions in her life, feelings she'd never experienced. Scary feelings, yet exhilarating — a daily discovery of how love works. The emotions Morgan caused were anything but familial. How had she allowed herself to become involved in such a tangle? Soon she would leave the captain's care and have nothing left but memories.

Shortly before dusk, she straightened from pinning a dish towel to the clothesline when she heard the shout, "Man the decks!"

Pilar's sewing fell to her lap as she stood to peer toward the wheelhouse. "I don't see anything." By now the other women had gathered around her.

Amelia pointed. "There's another paddle wheeler pulling alongside us."

Silence gripped the women. Amelia's pulse pounded in her throat as she anxiously strained to see the arrivals. Brown? The knot in her throat seized. Moments passed, and her curiosity got the better of her. Dropping the dishcloth she held, she rushed to the lower deck. Others followed.

"Are we racing?" Bunny asked.

A grin broke across Amelia's face. "I hope so!" That would be too much to hope for. First the showboat, and now a race between two paddle steamers! Nothing more exciting — or dangerous. Tales of exploding steamboat boilers abounded, yet Amelia had heard that captains took delight in the sport.

"I hope not," Pilar called above the sudden groaning engine.

"A race!" Amelia could barely contain her excitement. She'd never seen a steamboat race and never once dreamed she would be a part of one!

She rushed up to the pilothouse and burst inside to find Morgan and Captain Jean Louis clearly enjoying themselves. "Are we racing?" She scurried to peer out at the second boat that was now gaining ground on the *Mississippi Lady*.

"No," Jean Louis stated calmly. He glanced toward Morgan, and they broke into roguish grins. "Just blowing the cobwebs out of the engine."

The boilers heated up. Black smoke and sparks belched from the *Mississippi Lady*'s tall stacks as she cut a wide path of boiling white froth through the water.

"Go below!" Morgan shouted over the din as the pace continued to pick up.

"Oh, Morgan!" She sobered. "Are you sure it isn't Austin Brown trying to trick us?" There had been no tangible evidence to indicate Brown was pursuing them, but everybody aboard knew that he wouldn't accept defeat so easily.

Morgan shook his head. "It isn't Brown. Now go below."

The two steamboats shot down the river, keeping pace with each other. Amelia's pulse quickened as the *Mississippi Lady* began to quake and strain from bow to stern.

"Amelia!" Morgan roared.

"I'm *going!*" She would miss the fun, but she would go. Her gaze fixed on the new vessel. The *Mississippi Lady* churned the waters, picking up speed. Her steps paused at the doorway, her eyes focused on the race.

The two paddle wheelers struggled side by side, their stacks expelling plumes of black smoke into the air.

Ryder and Henry frantically shoved wood into the boilers, bumping into each other as they fed the fire.

"Did I tell you about the time I held the horns?" Jean Louis shouted as he deftly steered the boat through the churning waters.

"Did you retain the honor?" Morgan called back.

"Four years in a row!"

Amelia glanced quizzically over her shoulder at Morgan. "The horns?" She had her hand on the door handle. She was going to obey Morgan — but the race — a tiny second more and she would leave.

Morgan glanced her way. "Holding the horns is a coveted award among river pilots. The horns are a gilded rack of deer antlers — the symbol of the speed king. The captain who wins the trophy mounts it in his pilot-house or the most prominent place on his ship."

Amelia bestowed an admiring grin on Captain Jean Louis, and he winked at her. "Watch this."

The old boat groaned under the building pressure as the two paddle wheelers came around a bend.

Jumping up and down now, Amelia howled with delight as Henry and Ryder pumped more wood into the boiler. "Yes!" Amelia clutched Morgan's arm. "We're pulling ahead!"

The decks of the *Mississippi Lady* vibrated as the stern slowly inched ahead of the other boat. She was running full throttle now, and white steam poured from the tops of the ships' stacks. Boiling white froth faded into long white streaks as they cut through the mucky water.

Suddenly the race was over as quickly as it had begun.

The *Mississippi Lady* shot ahead, taking the lead, and the other boat dropped behind.

Sounding a victory blast on the horn, Jean Louis laughed merrily as the *Mississippi Lady* sailed on down the river.

With a shout, Amelia threw her arms around Morgan's neck and hugged him. This was absolutely the most fun she'd had since she and her sisters dropped wild onions in the mission well!

"Wasn't the race the most exciting thing you've ever done?" Amelia exclaimed as the women prepared for bed that night.

"Do you know how many people are killed by exploding boilers?" Elizabeth asked. "The race was insane. Men acting like little boys."

"Oh pooh," Amelia muttered. "The boiler didn't explode, did it? Captain Jean Louis wouldn't do anything to get us hurt."

"Captain Jean Louis is a man, isn't he?" Elizabeth stretched out on her bunk. "And a man can be thoughtless when adventure calls." She deftly filled a cigarette paper with tobacco. "Caught up by the prospect of a race, men have been known to be downright reckless at times."

"Well, the boiler didn't explode." Amelia shrugged and looked away. "So let's talk about something else." She glanced back again when she heard a soft rustling sound as Elizabeth withdrew a pouch of tobacco from her pocket. Amelia's heart quickened when she recognized the brown pouch with the red writing. Morgan had purchased it from the gypsy.

A wave of jealousy knotted Amelia's stomach. A small voice warned her to look away, to drop the subject while she could still salvage her pride. But a strong urge compelled her to stare accusingly into Elizabeth's cool eyes.

Elizabeth broke eye contact to sprinkle tobacco onto a cigarette paper that she was holding with steady fingers. With a practiced move, she locked her teeth onto the drawstring and tugged the pouch closed with one hand. She casually rolled the cigarette and stuck it between her lips, full lips that quirked at the corners in a mocking smile. Grudgingly, Amelia stared at Elizabeth's mouth. She imagined Morgan and Elizabeth embracing and kissing in the dark corner beneath the stairway, the same dark corner where Morgan had kissed her not so long ago. She suffered such a thrust of pain in her chest that for a long moment she couldn't draw a breath.

Please, God, don't let me care so much. I'm doing my best to remain friendly to Elizabeth. It seemed as though the Almighty didn't want her to like this woman, who at times seemed very lonely.

"Where were you when all the excitement was going on?" The words were out before she could stop them.

Elizabeth raised an eyebrow as she struck a match. "None of your business where I was." She held the flame to her cigarette and drew on it until the tip glowed a bright red.

The tension grew until the room felt suffocating with humidity and smoke. Faith shot to her feet to stand between Amelia and Elizabeth. "See how nice the lace looks on the curtains?"

Amelia didn't blink. "Very nice."

Elizabeth shrugged. "What's the big whooping deal about a boat race? I can whistle and eat soda crackers at the same time."

The girls' heads swiveled in unison to gape at her.

Taking a slow drag off her cigarette, Elizabeth mocked, "Surprise!"

Amelia shook her head. She had never met a man who could do that.

"Well, I can."

"Prove it." Amelia wasn't about to take Elizabeth's word for it. Eating crackers and whistling. At the same time? She didn't think so.

Elizabeth rolled off the bunk and sat up. "Get me some crackers."

Amelia left the cabin and was back in record time with a handful of crackers. The women clustered around Elizabeth's bunk.

"Okay. Prove it." Amelia knew that Elizabeth couldn't. She was showing off again.

Elizabeth methodically stacked four crackers on top of one another and then bit into them, her eyes locked defiantly with Amelia's.

"She can't," Amelia assured the others. "She's bragging, as usual."

Elizabeth ate the four crackers, chewing slowly and then polished off four more.

"Whistle," Amelia said.

"What do you want me to whistle?"

"Anything," Ria said.

"Okay." Elizabeth began to whistle a spirited rendition of "Dixie."

"Good grief," Amelia breathed, fascinated by the spray of crumbs spewing from Elizabeth's mouth. The woman was flat out whistling after eating eight crackers.

"That's really good," Faith said.

"I told you I could do it." Elizabeth settled back to finish her smoke.

Amelia returned to her pallet. She tried whistling "Dixie" under her breath but gave up when she saw the others staring at her strangely.

"Maybe we're not like you, Elizabeth." The innuendo was clear. Amelia wasn't proud of herself for pointing it out, but it was true. They weren't like Elizabeth, especially when it came to men.

"You're right. You aren't like me in the least. I was married once."

The silence in the room turned deafening.

"Married." Amelia found her voice first. "You were not!"

"Yes, I was."

Amelia's eyes widened with sudden understanding. Well, no wonder Morgan preferred her! She knew everything there was to know when it came to men. "Oh?" She turned wary. It wouldn't be above Elizabeth to fib to them. "If that's true, where's your husband?"

Pain briefly crossed Elizabeth's face. "None of your business."

"Oh no you don't," Amelia countered. "You can't just tell us you were married and then brush it off with a 'never mind.' If you are married, where's your husband?"

"I'm no longer married," Elizabeth said. "So forget it."

"Why not?" Amelia glanced at the others. If they weren't going to call Elizabeth's hand on this, then she would. "Were you so rotten and mean that he ran off and left you?"

Nervous giggles broke out among the others.

"My husband is dead."

Elizabeth's tone was so grave that Amelia

was tempted to believe her. Then she reminded herself that the woman was an expert at deception. She'd like nothing better than to make her look like a fool.

"Boo hoo. I'm sorry. You should have told us," she mocked.

"It isn't anything I care to talk about."

Amelia raised her brows at the others. Elizabeth could certainly lay it on thick.

"Elizabeth," Pilar chided. "Death is very sad. You shouldn't tease about such things."

"I'm not teasing. My husband is dead."

For a moment no one could think of a single thing to say. Finally, Amelia broke the strained silence. "Elizabeth, is this really true? Were you really married and your husband died?"

"My husband is dead," she repeated, more softly now.

The mood in the room changed. Rising from her pallet, Amelia confronted her. "Elizabeth —"

Elizabeth shrugged off her efforts. "I don't want your pity."

Amelia was silent for a moment. She glanced at the others and then back to Elizabeth. "Well, it would be all right if you wanted to talk about it." It felt strange being nice to Elizabeth. Not bad, but strange. Amelia examined her conscience and decided that she could be decent, providing Elizabeth was telling the truth.

When Amelia turned to go back to her bunk, Elizabeth said softly, "We had been married five months when the war started. Marcus didn't believe in bloodshed. Our church prohibited his taking another man's life, so when he was asked to fight, he declined, holding to his beliefs. The men of our community were angered by his refusal. After that, we were considered outcasts."

Years of bitterness and resentment tumbled out of Elizabeth, word on top of word, as if by voicing her past she would be cleansed of the terrible ache she had lived with for too long.

"We farmed twenty acres outside of town, so we were busy most of the time. We were so young and in love that what went on with the rest of the world didn't matter to us." Her eyes filled with love. "We were so crazy in love. Marcus worked the fields, and I took care of the house."

A tear rolled from the corner of her eye, and she self-consciously wiped it aside.

"It was raining the day it happened. Marcus was reading a farm journal, and I had just taken an apple pie out of the oven." She paused, apparently recalling how much her husband loved pie. "When we heard the horses, we thought it was a neighbor coming to visit, although that would have been unusual. Folks didn't much care for anyone who wasn't willing to fight for their cause."

Her features hardened, looking more like the Elizabeth that Amelia knew. "Some men, members of a vigilante group, met me at the door. I asked them what they wanted, and they cursed me, saying that Marcus was spineless for not fighting. They called him a coward and a disgrace to his brotherhood. When Marcus came to the door to see who was there, the men shoved me aside and dragged my husband out to the barn and hanged him there."

Pilar gasped softly.

"I tried to stop them. I pleaded and cried, but they wouldn't listen. After Marcus was dead, they torched the house and the outbuildings. When they left," Elizabeth whispered, "I cut Marcus's body down and buried him. I stayed in what was left of the cabin for three days, not knowing what to do or where to turn. I was paralyzed with fear that the men would come back and do the same to me. The nights were cold, and it rained during the days. Finally, a neighbor to the east saw the smoke and came to investigate. When he learned what had happened, he and his wife took pity on me and let me stay with them until I could find a place to go."

"What about your parents?" Mahalia asked quietly. "Couldn't you have gone to them?"

Elizabeth shook her head. "My father died before I was born. Mother was young and scared, and she didn't know what to do. We went to live with a cousin in Virginia. Cousin June died when I was fourteen. I had no one but Marcus."

"What about your husband's parents?" Amelia asked.

Elizabeth shook her head. "There was only his father, who was in such poor health I couldn't go to him and tell him about Marcus. The shock would have killed him."

Sliding off her cot, Belicia knelt beside her. "I am so sorry, Elizabeth. We had no idea."

Elizabeth lifted her head defiantly. "I don't need your sympathy. I'm a survivor. Pray for the men who did this to Marcus. Ask that their souls will burn forever in hell." Wiping the tears from her eyes, she straightened, her face showing none of her recent emotion. "I'm not the only one here who hasn't lived a fairy-tale life."

A few nodded. Mira said, "I, too, have suffered at the hands of others."

Mira reached for Elizabeth's tobacco pouch. "I'll fix you a smoke, Elizabeth."

A hint of warmth entered Elizabeth's eyes when Bunny helped wipe away her lingering tears. "Thank you, Mira, Bunny."

"You're welcome, and if you ever need anything, you can come to me. You can trust me," Bunny vowed.

Clearing her throat, Amelia added softly, "You have all of our friendships, if you want." Knowing Morgan's preference, it would hurt to befriend this woman, but Amelia could do it. "Blessed are the peacemakers: for they shall be called the children of God" — Sister Agnes would have quoted that verse.

The eyes of the two women met in silent understanding. Attitudes would be easier between them now.

Reaching for Bunny's hand, Faith smiled. "Well, the one nice thing about all this is that we're sort of like a family now."

The others murmured their poignant agreement. Amelia knew their paths were sure to take opposite directions when they reached New Orleans, but from this moment on they would be together in spirit.

Amelia was up before the sun the next morning. The journey would be over shortly, and she would be in New Orleans — on her own. Grabbing her fishing pole, she went to the back of the deck to get in a few hours of fishing before breakfast. The old engine had been kerplunking along smoothly before she noticed an odd noise.

Setting her pole aside, she ventured to the boiler area, where she found Morgan and Jean Louis bent over, shaking their heads and muttering.

"Is something wrong?" she asked, trying to peer over Morgan's shoulder.

"Trouble with the pressure lines," the captain murmured.

Amelia stepped closer, fixed on the boiler. "Can you fix it?"

"Yes, but it means an unscheduled stop."

"Which does not give you license to leave this boat," Morgan reminded her.

The two men rolled up their sleeves and were soon immersed in repairing the boiler.

A few of the women dropped by to view the goings-on, but in general, life aboard the *Mississippi Lady* proceeded at a normal pace.

The boat struggled to the next landing, where the captain moored it.

Amelia returned to fishing, but her heart wasn't in it. She wanted to stop time, to spend every day — every hour — aboard the *Mississippi Lady* with her new family. If Abigail and Anne-Marie were here, life would be perfect. Perhaps if she spoke with Jean Louis her wish could be granted. The boat could use more feminine help.

Dinnertime came and went. Mahalia had taken Morgan and Jean Louis their plates because they seemed too busy to eat with the others.

The sun climbed higher in the sky. Amelia slipped off her shoes and pushed up the sleeves of her dress. The day was warm and muggy. Sweat trickled down the sides of her face.

Another hour passed, and it was too hot to fish. Abandoning her pole, she went to the water bucket for a cool drink. The delay didn't bother her. That meant she would spend longer on the river. The thought made her happy. A couple more nights, a few more hours with Morgan.

Lifting her head, she blotted the drops of water above her upper lip on her sleeve as her eyes focused on the old boiler. The men looked completely absorbed in trying to repair it now.

She let the dipper drop back into the bucket and then sidled along the railing to edge her way toward the bow of the boat.

Bunny was there, hanging out the wash.

"Hi," she mumbled around the clothespins wedged between her front teeth.

"Hi."

"Thought you were fishing."

Amelia helped her pin another shirt to the line strung between two wooden beams. "I am. I got thirsty and came down for a drink of water. The boat is awfully close to the bank, isn't it?"

"It's been drifting all morning. Guess the captains are preoccupied with the boiler."

Bunny pinned another garment. "I think we're all jumpy. We're so close to freedom that I can't bear the thought of anything going wrong."

"Nothing will go wrong. Most likely Austin Brown gave up days ago and turned back, if he was following us in the first place. I've been watching close, and I haven't seen a sign of any boat following."

"Maybe. What's the first thing you're going to do when we're safe?"

"Buy my ticket back to Mercy Flats. And you?"

"I don't know. I don't have anywhere in particular to go. I've been alone since I was fifteen. My grandmother died, and I never knew my parents."

"How would you feel about coming to Mercy Flats with me? The convent is very old, and the sisters are aging as well. I'm certain they would welcome each and every one of you into their arms."

"Goodness." Bunny's hand paused. "Go with you to Mercy Flats?"

"Sure." The thought had come out of nowhere, but Amelia quickly warmed to the idea. She would love to take the others back to the mission with her. It wasn't likely Jean Louis needed more help aboard — and she didn't know with any certainty about Abigail and Anne-Marie's fate. She could only continue to pray that their rescuers were as kind as Morgan. "Can you think of a reason why that wouldn't be the best solution? I'll invite the others after supper. I know one or two have homes, but you and I have bonded, don't you agree?" Other than Elizabeth, Amelia couldn't think of one she hadn't come to love. And with time, she would like Elizabeth. She would make herself like the woman.

"Oh my." Bunny picked up a pair of bloomers. "What a comforting thought. I know I will gladly accept your invitation. I've been lying awake at night wondering what I would do and where I would go. Work is scarce because of the war, and I could imagine myself back on the streets, exactly where I was when Austin Brown and his thugs abducted me. Then you came along and I had hope again." Bunny turned. "Amelia?"

"Yes?"

"Thank you." Bunny leaned to hug her. "Thank you so much."

"Don't thank me. Thank God." Amelia flashed a grin. "He thinks of everything."

Long after the women had gone to bed, Amelia heard the sound of the old Bolton and Watt sputter a couple of times and then spring to life. Too sleepy to respond, she turned to her side and murmured, "Thank You, God."

Sleepy voices around her murmured the sentiment. The boat's deck vibrated as the sound of the steam engine coming to life lulled Amelia back to sleep with a desolate thought.

The last leg of the journey had begun.

Midmorning the following day, Amelia's worst fear materialized. A boat was following now, staying well behind but keeping pace with the paddle wheeler. Austin Brown. Amelia knew she wasn't mistaken about the swift, newer cargo ship that was now trailing the paddle wheeler.

Low-hanging clouds in the west threatened imminent rain when Morgan joined her at the railing.

"Good morning," she murmured. "Do you see what I see?"

"We see him. He joined us about an hour ago. You'd better round up the women and go below." Amelia noted his grave tone, the tight set of his lips. Her heart started to thump. "What happens now?"

"Now we fight."

She reached over and caught his hand, despair filling her. "Morgan . . ."

"Go below, Amelia. Jean Louis and I will handle this." When she turned, he caught her hand and drew her back. Holding her tightly, he whispered against her ear. "Don't try to help. This could get rough."

She buried her face in the front of his shirt, breathing deeply of his familiar scent, fearing this would be the last time he held her. A terrifying sense of doom squeezed her windpipe. Brown would have a whole boatload of thugs to help recapture the women. Morgan and Jean Louis would be only two against many. The odds were insurmountable.

His hold tightened briefly before he released her. "Gather the women and go below. There's a stretch of river coming up shortly. There is where Brown will make his move."

Tipping her face upward, Morgan gave her a brief kiss. "You look pretty in the morning light."

"Morgan, I have something to say."

"Is there a time when you don't?"

"Don't say no until you've heard me out." Avoiding his gaze, she took a deep breath. "I want to leave the boat immediately. Have Jean Louis pull closer to the shoreline, and I'll get out."

He released her and gently turned her toward the pilothouse. "That's not an option. Now go below."

Shaking her head, she refused to budge. By now the other women apparently noted the following boat and started to gather. Pilar walked to Morgan and Amelia standing at the railing. "It's Brown, isn't it?"

"It's Brown," Morgan acknowledged. "Pilar, get the women below and take Amelia with you."

"No." The young woman's eyes turned grim. "I overheard what Amelia said, and I agree. Have Jean Louis move the boat closer to shore, and we will get off. Brown wants us, not you and Jean Louis. It isn't right that you and the captain risk your life any longer for what appears to be inevitable."

The other women nodded mute support. Bunny spoke up. "What Pilar says is true.

Brown doesn't want you; he wants us."

Elizabeth stepped to the front and faced Morgan. "If you and Jean Louis are killed, which you will be with the odds against you, we will meet the same fate as if you'd walked away. Let us off the boat, and we'll try and make a break for it. I promise I'll do my best to keep the girls safe."

"Elizabeth." Morgan shifted his stance. "How long have you known me?"

"Long enough to know you're pigheaded and stubborn as a mule, but this time your compassion is going to get you killed."

"For once, I agree with Elizabeth." Amelia reached to take Elizabeth's hand in a sign of unity. She could argue with herself all she wanted, but Morgan and Elizabeth's "friendship" was a fact, one she had to get used to. She didn't intend to stand by and see Morgan shot because of her. She loved him far too much to see any harm come to him because of her foolish nature. It occurred to her that perhaps she might have fallen for a rogue — a man who would carelessly share his kisses with two women! She straightened. She was going to point that out to the scoundrel the moment this new crisis was over — if she could still talk.

Morgan took Amelia and Elizabeth by their forearms and ushered them to the foot of the steps. "Go below." He turned and motioned for the others to follow.

One by one the women slipped past, murmuring heartfelt warnings to take care.

Periodically, Amelia moved to the porthole, watching Austin Brown draw closer. Elizabeth and the others were working on the new curtains, going about their business as though their world wasn't about to come to an end, as if the pretty gingham would actually hang at the porthole windows.

Amelia stepped from her observation spot, and Bunny took her place at the window. Seconds passed before Amelia's cheeks flushed with excitement. "Come see! There's a huge boat coming toward us carrying hundreds of people. Come see!"

The women dropped their sewing and ran to the porthole, crowding around the clouded glass. Niles's voice drifted from above their heads.

"Lord A'mighty," he murmured. "What a beautiful sight."

"What is it?" Amelia stood on her tiptoes to see.

Morgan's voice followed. "I can't imagine."

Someone aboard the other boat shouted, cupping his hands to his mouth to be heard above the clatter of engines.

"What?" Henry yelled back.

Squeezing through a hole, Amelia elbowed her way to the front.

"Over! War! Have you heard the war is over?"

"Eh?" Niles cupped his hand to his ear.

"War is over!"

Amelia turned to Ria, breaking into a smile. "The war is over. That's what he said. The war is *over*!"

Morgan leaned over the railing, shouting. "The war's over?"

Waving and jumping up and down, the caller shouted back. "Lee surrendered to Grant! War's over!"

"When?"

"On the ninth at Appomattox! Lee surrendered to Grant!"

"The ninth," Morgan shouted. "What month is this? April?"

"Late April!"

Bedlam broke out aboard the *Mississippi Lady.* The women raced to the deck as the crew celebrated the stunning news. The war was over! Praise God!

Jumping up and down, the women cried and hugged each other. Words like "I can hardly believe it!" filled the air. Even Elizabeth was spotted lifting the hem of her shirttail to wipe away tears of apparent joy.

As the huge vessel pulled even with the *Mississippi Lady,* the mood turned somber.

Hundreds of discharged, ragtag soldiers leaned wearily against the rail, staring back with lifeless eyes.

The man who had been doing all the shouting leaned over the railing and shouted again, "Have you not heard? Lincoln is dead!"

"Dead?" Morgan called back. "When?"

"Week and a half ago. Ford's Theatre. Shot in the head! The funeral train is taking his body to Springfield, Illinois."

President Lincoln was dead. The war was over, and a man of gentle spirit, a man who had made himself needlessly accessible at times, a man who was unswerving in his goal of restoring and preserving the Union, President Abraham Lincoln, was dead.

"Where are you going?" Morgan called.

"Home," the man shouted back.

"Good luck to you, then." Morgan waved, and the other man returned the gesture as the boat continued downstream.

Amelia raced to hug Morgan tightly around the neck, nearly taking him to his knees in her jubilance. "Thank you . . . oh, thank you for saving us to witness such glorious news!"

"Thank the good Lord. We're going to

need His blessing."

Hester came with Bunny close behind, and pretty soon Morgan had women hanging all over him, showering him with their gratitude.

Amelia stood beside Elizabeth, smiling at the exhibition. Her head spun with the news.

Morgan's eyes found her above all the commotion, and somehow her gaze told him more than she ever could have.

Was she showing too much gratitude?

Yes, but by now it was obvious she adored him. Anyone with sight would know that.

TEN

Morgan reached out and caught Amelia by the arm as she tried to sidestep him when the cheering faded away. "You're supposed to be below."

"You couldn't possibly think I would stay below when something this meaningful happens." She struggled out of his hold and turned to walk away, but he stopped her. Brown was keeping a safe distance behind the *Mississippi Lady*. The river curve was approaching. There would be precious little time to talk in a brief while.

Morgan knew that his distorted relationship with Elizabeth worried Amelia, and she had every right to suspect him of being a rogue. He didn't deny that her feelings had come to matter to him, a recognition that he didn't fight. If they reached New Orleans, he was going to explain to her about his relationship with Elizabeth. With the war over, it no longer mattered if she knew his role in it. Oddly enough, he had come to gain her trust, and he seriously doubted she would find it necessary to reveal his and Elizabeth's purpose. He found the thought of exploring his and Amelia's growing attraction energizing.

Energizing? A strange choice of words. Any other he might use to describe his feelings for her was even more disturbing to him.

Dark, threatening clouds now blocked the setting sun. Everyone aboard admitted that nerves were stretched. The river bend had failed to materialize, but Jean Louis assured Morgan over supper that it would. Morgan's memory served him well.

Morgan scooped another mound of potatoes onto his plate. "We should have reached that bend two hours ago."

"The broken boiler has thrown your timing off." Jean Louis reached for the salt.

"Still, it will be dark soon. I'd just as soon fight this battle in broad daylight."

"Humph." Niles heaped gravy on a split biscuit. "I'd just as soon not fight it."

Izzy leaned over and gave his hand a little pat.

Shortly after supper, Amelia was in the galley with Mahalia and Izzy when the first roll of thunder sounded in the distance. Izzy glanced up, concern creasing her brow. "Lawsy, I was hoping we'd reach New Orleans with nary a storm. Better batten down the hatches, girls."

While Izzy locked the cupboards, Amelia and Mahalia put away everything breakable.

Morgan appeared in the doorway. "It looks like heavy weather moving in. Take the proper precautions."

Lightning forked the sky, followed by the crackling sound of thunder. The storm was closer now, moving in fast.

Faith ran to help Bunny gather in the wash, which was flapping wildly in the rising wind, while Niles and Ryder secured the boat.

A heavy wind gust sent ropes skittering across the deck. Jagged lightning streaked the sky, followed by peals of explosive thunder.

The men donned oil slickers, shouting to hear one another above the rising fury.

"I can't swim," Pilar reminded Amelia as they hurried along the deck. "What if the boat capsizes?"

"It won't. It's too big." Actually, she had no idea if the boat would stay afloat, but they had enough to worry about without adding a sinking vessel.

"But what if it does?"

"Then we'll get wet. Don't worry, I'll be right there beside you," Amelia promised, "exactly like when we had to escape the *Black Widow.*"

"But it wasn't storming then!"

Chaos broke out as the storm vented its full fury. The *Mississippi Lady* rocked back and forth as sheets of rain pelted the cabin window.

The women huddled close, listening with mounting terror as rain lashed the portholes. "If Brown doesn't get us, this storm will," Mahalia promised.

"Shush!" Amelia reached to comfort a quaking Pilar.

The boat shook and creaked back and forth in the heavy waves as lightning and thunder now came on the heels of each other.

When she couldn't stand it any longer, Amelia slipped away, returning to the pilothouse where both Morgan and Captain Jean Louis were fighting the wheel.

"Where are the others?" Jean Louis shouted.

"Below."

"Better tie yourselves to the bunk. It's gonna be a bad one!"

Morgan fought the wheel, spinning it to a

sharp right to keep it in the channel. "Amelia."

"Yes?"

His eyes left the river long enough to find hers. "Be careful!"

She nodded. "You too."

Minutes later a drenched Amelia raced back to the cabin and banged on the cabin door. "Captain wants us to tie ourselves down!"

Fear dominated eyes. Tears rolled down Bunny's cheeks. "Can't we go above and all be together when we go dow —"

Amelia cut off Bunny's words. "I know the captains will hate it, but I don't want to drown in the bottom of this boat. Let's go." The young woman broke and headed for the door.

Ria and Bunny followed close on Amelia's heels.

The women poured out and held tightly to one other as they made their way along the slippery walkway. Rain blinded Amelia, who grasped Pilar's hand tightly and led the way.

As they reached the galley, a violent gust of wind nearly blew her off her feet. "I have to see about Izzy and Henry. Someone go after Niles and Ryder!"

Screaming, Pilar clutched tightly to

Amelia's skirt as the two women fought to retain their footing. Thunder crashed overhead, and the boat rolled on the heavy waves. Above, in the pilothouse, Amelia could hear Morgan shouting to her.

"We're coming up there!" she shouted back.

A fierce gust shattered the row of galley windows as the others scrambled up the steps.

Gasping, Pilar grabbed for Amelia and pointed to the old curtains being whipped to pieces in the wind.

"We can't do anything about them," Amelia called. "They'll be taken down soon anyway."

Breaking away, Pilar ran to the galley steps and began to climb them, seemingly intent on rescuing the tattered fabric. Pilar had once said that she was taught never to waste anything. Nothing.

"Pilar, no!" Amelia shouted. The wind and rain were ferocious now, battering the old boat violently. Old curtains were not worth a life.

The young woman climbed the ladder and burst inside. Following her up the steps, Amelia slipped, slashing her knee open as she tried to reach her.

Pilar jerked down a curtain, but the old

boat was rocking back and forth so violently, it was impossible to keep her footing. She fell, tumbling to the wall.

"Leave them," Amelia shouted, trying to pull the young woman to her feet. "The new ones are nearly through!"

"No! To be wasteful is sin!" The two women battled the wind to save the curtains. Hail began to fall, tiny spheres at first, and then vicious ice pellets rained from above. The sky turned a peculiar greenish color. Amelia lost her balance again and skidded across the floor of the galley.

Crawling back to Pilar, she latched onto the hem of her skirt, trying to pull her away from the broken glass.

"We have to go, Pilar! Leave the curtains!"

Another heavy wave hit the boat, tipping it sideways. Both women screamed.

They clung together, and Amelia's heart sank as wave after powerful wave swamped the boat. They were going to drown if they didn't get to higher ground.

Locking hands, Amelia started to crawl, prepared to drag her friend to safety. Pulling the young woman out of the galley, Amelia dragged her down the steps as the storm raged.

Muddy waters lashed the decks with vengeance when Amelia began inching her way to the pilothouse steps, dragging Pilar behind her. By all that was holy, she wasn't going to give Morgan another thing to worry about. He and Captain Jean Louis had enough trouble trying to keep the boat afloat, and she was quite certain the two men didn't give a fig about hangings.

When she realized what she was thinking, she squealed, lifting her face to the storm to let out a gleeful shout. By golly, she did have it! She didn't know where or when she'd gotten it, but she had it now! Responsibility. Integrity. How sweet it was!

Her joy was short lived as she felt wave after wave crash against the sides of the boat. Water and hail were coming from every direction as the two women struggled down the steps, trying to hold on to each other.

"Don't let go of me!" Pilar screamed, hysterical now.

"I won't . . ." Amelia bit her lip, tightening her hold. "I'll hold you! We need to get to the pilothouse quickly." The people aboard now held a snug place in her heart, and if the boat went down, she wanted to go with her new family.

Wind and lightning pounded the boat while another wave surged. Suddenly Amelia and Pilar were catapulted through the air and swept over the railing.

When Amelia hit the water, her breath was momentarily knocked out of her.

Waves crashed over her head. The muddy Mississippi had become a dark, churning demon as thunder and lightning rolled across the sky.

Morgan fought the wheel and helplessly watched the events taking place below him. Even as he shouted to Amelia, he realized she couldn't hear him. Why were she and the others fighting their way to the pilot-house? Hadn't he distinctly told her to keep the others below? His breath caught when he saw a wave hurl two of the women overboard.

Jean Louis motioned him toward the women, and the captain took the wheel. Morgan felt a wave of panic as he raced to the lower deck, shouting Amelia's name.

Thrashing about in the water, Amelia called for Pilar, straining to catch a gasp of air. "Pilar! Pilar!"

A wave engulfed her, taking her under again. Surfacing, she spat out a mouthful of dirty water. She couldn't see anything but black, rolling water with a glimpse of a pale green sky. Hail beat down amid bursts of thunderous explosions.

Lightning split the sky. Amelia spotted a boat in the distance.

The *Mississippi Lady*! "Here!" she shouted, waving. "Over here!"

She cried out for Pilar again, struggling to swim against the swift current. It was useless. She was a strong swimmer, but the water's pull was too strong.

Her head slipped under.

The boat drew closer, angling alongside the figure thrashing about in the water.

"Can you swim to the boat?" Amelia heard a male voice call.

Wiping the water out of her eyes, she tried to focus. Where was the voice coming from? Pilar? Dear God, where was Pilar? Pilar couldn't swim!

"Over here!" the voice shouted.

"Morgan?" Was it Morgan's voice calling to her? Had he seen her go overboard? Hope sprang to life within her, and she began to thrash through the water, trying to reach him.

"Morgan?" she shouted.

"Over here! Swim to the boat!"

Blindly, she struck out in the direction of his voice, fighting the wind and the rain.

"That's good," the voice encouraged. "Just a few feet more!"

Gasping for breath, Amelia swam harder.

She'd swum often with her sisters, Abigail and Anne-Marie, but they had never attempted to swim in conditions like this.

"Where are you?" she gasped.

"You're close, very close!"

Amelia reached out, grasping at thin air. "Where? Where? I can't see you!"

"Just a few feet more!" the commanding voice urged. "Come on, you can do it!"

With every ounce of strength left in her, Amelia battled the elements. Twice, heavy waves swamped her, but she surfaced with a new vengeance. "Pilar! Where is Pilar?" she called, her voice weaker now.

"She's aboard!" the voice shouted back.

Relief flooded Amelia. *Thank You, God, oh, thank You, God! Pilar is safe.* They would both be saved.

Blindly extending her hand, she prayed there would be a force to meet her.

Strong fingers gripped her arm, lending her the strength she needed to push through the last few feet to the boat.

She wanted to cry out when she felt his hand close over hers. For all their differences, he cared. Morgan cared whether she lived or died. She understood that he had thought enough of her to risk his life to save hers. *Oh, Morgan, you do care,* she thought when she was pulled from the water.

Someone threw a blanket around her shoulders as she wiped the muddy water from her eyes, gasping for breath.

"Oh, Morgan —" Her voice died an instant death when her eyes began to focus.

It wasn't Morgan standing before her. It was Austin Brown.

With a wicked smile, Théodore Austin Brown raked a lecherous look down her trembling body. "Hello, lovey. Terrible storm, eh?"

ELEVEN

Amelia stared into her enemy's sinister black eyes. No, not now! Not when they were so close to victory.

Trailing a long, slender finger down her muddied cheek, Brown glared at her, his lips curled with contempt. "Surely you didn't think you and that reckless, misguided young Union officer could outwit me, did you?"

Her eyes searched her surroundings. "Pilar. Where's Pilar?"

His brows lifted questioningly. "Pilar? Why, I don't believe I've seen your friend recently." He threw his head back and laughed. Then, just as quickly, his eyes turned dangerously cold. "I fear the little fishes will be feasting on her about now, dear one."

Flying at him, Amelia struck out, pummeling him angrily. He had lied to her! He had made her believe Pilar was safely aboard.

Enraged, she struck at him over and over, but his amusement only increased. "You little fool! You and Kane thought you were so clever," he sneered. "You thought you could escape me."

Grasping her roughly by the shoulders, he shook her until her teeth rattled.

"Fool!" he shouted above the rain and the thunder. "Silly, mindless fool! No one escapes Austin Brown!"

A shot rang out, and blood spurted from Brown's shoulder. Stunned, he momentarily released his hold on Amelia.

Whirling, Amelia broke from him and raced toward the railing as a hail of gunfire sprayed the boat.

"Seize her!" Brown shouted.

Men sprang forward to grab her, but Amelia scrambled over the boat's railing and dove back into the churning water.

Gunshots peppered the air over Amelia's head as she thrashed about, her eyes searching for the *Mississippi Lady.*

"Here!" Faith's voice came to her through the din of rain and gunfire. "Over here!"

Swimming toward the voice, Amelia felt herself becoming disoriented. Thunder and lightning raged overhead.

"Here! No! You're going the wrong way!" Faith shouted.

"Come on, girl, look where you're going!" Ryder shouted. "Over here!"

Ria's voice joined in. "Follow the sounds of our voices!"

Shots volleyed over Amelia's head as the occupants of the two boats fired on one another.

Diving beneath the water, Amelia swam as hard as she could. Her head pounded and she thought her lungs would burst, but she swam on.

Surfacing periodically, she took deep gulps of air as her eyes frantically searched the turbulent waters.

A flare suddenly illuminated the sky, and she cried out with relief when she saw the *Mississippi Lady* only a few feet in front of her. With a desperate effort, she reached out and felt a hand latch onto hers, an incredibly strong hand that pulled her safely aboard.

This time it was Morgan's arms that enfolded her, holding her tightly as she clung to him.

"You are putting gray hairs on my head," he whispered gruffly.

Lifting her mouth to his, she succumbed to his kiss as shots whizzed over their heads.

"Oh, Amelia." Bunny rushed up to hug her as Morgan turned away and began firing on Austin's boat again.

The women ducked behind the galley, taking shelter as Morgan, Henry, Niles, and Ryder kept up a steady rain of bullets directed at Austin Brown's boat.

"Girl, you had us worried sick," Mahalia told her as the women huddled together tightly.

"I'm fine, but Pilar —" Amelia broke off in a sob, and her heart shattered at the thought of losing the young woman. She had trusted Amelia to save her, and Amelia had failed.

"What's wrong with me?"

Amelia glanced over to see Pilar grinning back at her as she tried to get warm beneath the blanket Elizabeth was holding.

Climbing over Ria, Amelia threw her arms around Pilar's neck, and the two women embraced.

"I thought —"

"I know. I thought you were too!"

Captain Jean Louis opened a window in the pilothouse. "Hang on, ladies — we're going to make a run for it!"

Thunder rent the sky as the captain took his place at the wheel. The others continued to fire when the old boat surged into motion.

Crouching low, Amelia made her way up to the wheelhouse.

"What can we do to help?" she asked as she entered, quickly closing the door behind her.

Captain Jean Louis swung the boat around slowly. "Lighten it up!" He shouted the order once more, and the men below began pitching cotton bales over the side.

The women raced to help. Amelia knew that the captain was sacrificing precious cargo for their safety. She whirled around and went to help. Two by two, the women hauled heavy bales to the railing and then pitched them overboard.

Amelia broke away and raced to help Morgan, who was now shoving wood into the old boiler. Niles and Henry worked feverishly at his side. The old boat began to pick up speed as the fire burned hotter.

"Amelia, go to the kitchen and get all the bacon sides you can find!"

Wheeling, Amelia ran to do as Morgan asked, wondering why he wanted bacon at a time like this. Even she didn't want bacon at the moment.

"Sure would like to have a peck of pitch

and pine knots right about now," Niles hollered.

In a race like this, all was fair, even though using highly combustible fuel such as bacon sides, pitch, and pine knots wasn't the safest thing to do.

The two boats whipped along in the storm with Austin Brown and his men in hot pursuit of the *Mississippi Lady.*

With cotton bales disposed of, the women ran to help feed the boilers. Pilar and Hester relieved Amelia as she returned from the galley with an armload of bacon sides.

Working as a team, the women broke up chairs and crates and anything they could find to fuel the boiler. Black smoke and sparks belched from the paddle wheeler's tall stacks as the two boats raced neck and neck.

Peeling off his shirt, Morgan tossed it aside. Sweat mingled with rain in heavy rivulets down his muscular back, bringing on a sheen that accentuated every ridge and valley of his powerful chest and back. For a moment Amelia stood and stared. Male workers at the mission had never removed their shirts.

Morgan glanced her way and grinned. "I suppose you've 'never in your life had so much excitement,' " he mimicked, echoing her now familiar phrase.

"No, and I hope I never will again!" she assured him, feeling a flush of embarrassment that she'd been caught gawking at him.

Frowning, she stepped aside when Elizabeth approached. Morgan tossed Elizabeth his rifle and bent to shove more bacon into the boiler.

Amelia stepped away, feeling helpless. There was nothing she could do. Elizabeth seemed as natural with a rifle in her hands as Izzy did holding a mixing bowl.

Elizabeth suddenly lowered the rifle and motioned for Amelia to come to her. Hurrying to Elizabeth's side, Amelia accepted the rifle, grasping it tightly, as Elizabeth positioned it on her shoulder. Elizabeth shouted above the din, "This thing will kick like a wild mule."

"I don't mind!" Amelia had never shot a rifle before, but she was eager to do anything she could to help defeat Austin Brown.

Standing behind her, Elizabeth steadied the rifle, saying firmly, "Easy now. Squeeze the trigger real slow-like."

Amelia took aim and squeezed. The gun exploded, rocking her backward on her feet, but the kick it gave her was exhilarating.

"Again," Elizabeth encouraged, and

Amelia fired off a second round.

The two ducked as the volley was returned, peppering the deck of the boat. The men aboard the *Mississippi Lady* were doing everything short of tying down the safety valve, which was too dangerous to consider. No one wanted to be reckless enough to explode the boiler.

Amelia popped up and fired again. "You know, Elizabeth. You're not so bad." She squeezed off another round.

"Well . . ." Elizabeth reached for a box of cartridges. "You take some getting used to, but once a person clears that hurdle, you're not so bad either."

"Faster!" Austin shouted. "You fools! They're getting away!"

The crew shoved wood into the boiler, sweat rolling down their backs. Austin clasped his bloody shoulder and paced the deck amid the thunder and lightning, his eyes searching the stormy night. His prey was within reach if these fools would only work harder!

"Faster!"

"We're doing the best we can!" a man shouted back.

White steam boiled from the stacks as the boat cut through the turbulent water.

"Not everything! Tie down the safety valve!" Austin shouted.

"But boss —"

"Tie down the valve!"

The pace remained frantic aboard the *Mississippi Lady.* The women worked alongside the men, piling more fuel into the old boiler. Amelia knew that at any moment the boiler could blow to smithereens. The crew labored at a feverish pace.

Wiping sweat and rain from her eyes, Amelia handed Morgan another pile of kindling. "The last of the galley benches," she shouted.

The two boats snaked around another bend in the river.

Elizabeth and Morgan worked side by side, she supporting his every move. When Amelia was caught staring, she noticed Elizabeth call Morgan's attention to the moment.

Pausing, he and Elizabeth shared a silent exchange.

"Amelia," Morgan called, motioning her to approach.

Walking toward him, her eyes locked with his. Her heart hammered against her ribs painfully. He was going to confirm her worst fears, that as soon as this was over, provided the good Lord allowed them to survive, he and Elizabeth would go to Washington. In the midst of chaos, he intended to add more. Elizabeth would warm his bed and have his children and live on the apple farm Morgan was so certain no woman wanted.

That wouldn't be the worst thing that could happen to Morgan Kane, but it was the rottenest thing that could happen to her. Elizabeth had known love once, and Amelia shouldn't begrudge her finding it again. She just wished Elizabeth's infatuation was with someone other than Morgan Kane.

When Amelia reached Morgan's side, he briefly enfolded her in his arms. He was shirtless and dirty and smelled of oil and sweat, but she didn't care in the least.

"There's something you need to know."

"No." Amelia shook her head. "You don't have to tell me," she whispered. "I know, and I've accepted it."

"You know so little," Elizabeth said, but not unkindly.

"It's all right, Elizabeth." Amelia faced her adversary, their eyes mirroring grudging respect.

"What's all right, you silly twit?" Elizabeth winked at Morgan.

"It's all right that you and Morgan are in love. I can understand why you would love him." Her eyes confirmed she shared the same emotion. Why? She didn't know. They'd met under the vilest of circumstances, and the brief time they had shared had been fraught with danger. Still, she knew. Without a doubt she knew that she would always love this man, regardless of the fact that he chose to marry another. Amelia now fully understood the power of love between one man and one woman.

"I don't love Morgan," Elizabeth said, sending Morgan a quick grin. "I'm fond of the big lout, but I'm certainly not in love with him."

Amelia's eyes darted to Morgan, her heart going out to him. "Oh, Morgan, she doesn't mean that!" Surely Elizabeth's candor had hurt his feelings dreadfully! Who could not love this man?

"Amelia." Morgan gently held her for a moment. "There is nothing between Elizabeth and me except work."

"Work?" Well, they needn't think she was a blind fool!

"Yes, work," Elizabeth said. "Morgan and I are working for the Union. We've been tracking Dov Lanigan for the past six months. When we met in Galveston, we had no idea that events would unfold the way they have."

Morgan picked up the story. "Dov Lanigan was due in Galveston about the time you and I got there, no doubt to pick up the other women. For some reason, Lanigan was delayed, but Elizabeth and I agreed we had no choice but to wait him out. Elizabeth was abducted the same night you were. Fortunately for me, you were both taken to the *Black Widow,* and you know the rest of the story."

"Then you're not a Union officer?"

Morgan smiled. "Elizabeth and I serve the Union, but . . . let's say, in a more discreet manner."

Amelia's anger surfaced. All this time, the two had led her to believe there was a love match between them. "Why didn't you tell me? The way you two have been acting toward each other, I thought —"

"We didn't tell you because you couldn't keep a secret if your life depended on it," Elizabeth said bluntly.

"I could . . ." Amelia caught the admission and then nodded sheepishly. "Not." She was glad they hadn't told her. Even she could concede that her impetuous tongue would probably have given them all away. Her gaze pivoted to Morgan. "Then you and Elizabeth . . . ?"

Morgan and Elizabeth smiled at each

other. "The times you saw us disappear together were only business meetings," Morgan said. "We've been trying to figure out what to do with the others once we reach New Orleans."

"Then you settled the problem." Elizabeth smiled, and it had the effect of softening her features. "It's very good of you, Amelia, to offer the others a home at the convent."

Amelia's eyes returned to the boat carrying Austin Brown and his scurrilous crew. "But now it looks as if none of us are going to make it," she whispered.

Morgan bent down and picked up the last of the kindling and shoved it into the boiler.

The two boats cut through the water, their big paddle wheels churning the muddy water into white froth.

The women gathered from both ends of the boat and huddled together as they awaited the outcome of the race. The *Mississippi Lady* was nearly out of wood and bacon. Niles, Ryder, and Henry slumped on the railing, their strength ebbing. Izzy stood beside her husband in the pouring rain.

Above in the pilothouse, Captain Jean Louis fought the wheel, but Amelia knew he couldn't hold on much longer. Her gaze focused on the white steam pouring from the stacks, aware neither boat could keep this pace forever. The old boilers were pushed to the limit and beyond.

Moving to stand in the shelter of Morgan's arms, Amelia allowed tears to slip from her lids, not for herself, because here in Morgan's arms she would die happy, but for Abigail and Anne-Marie and the sisters at the convent who would never know what had happened to her. Her loved ones would watch for her for the rest of their lives, never knowing she had lost her life trying to outrun Austin Brown and his villainous crew, who'd wanted to sell her to evil men — an act that would ultimately bring about doom to all.

She frowned. Chances were, no one would ever believe it if they did happen to conjure up such an unlikely scenario. The old boat vibrated beneath her feet, straining with effort.

Amelia started when a thunderous boom rocked the boat, followed by a second blast. Flying wreckage, scalding water, escaping steam, and cries of distress filled the air, and she felt herself being lifted up and flung into the churning, muddy Mississippi.

Bobbing to the surface, she fought the heavy waves, her eyes searching the littered waters. "Morgan!" she screamed.

"Over here!"

As her eyes cleared, she saw Izzy and Niles side by side, clinging to a floating piece of wood. In the distance, she heard Faith and Hester encouraging Ryder to stay afloat.

Bunny and Mahalia latched onto Henry and Pilar while the others struggled against the swift current.

"Is everyone accounted for?" someone shouted.

One by one, each began to call out his or her name. Niles, Izzy, Ryder, Henry, Hester, Faith, Mahalia, Bunny, Mira, Ria, Belicia, Auria, Pilar, Elizabeth, Morgan, Captain Jean Louis.

"Here!" Amelia confirmed. "What happened!"

"A boiler blew!" a voice called.

"Our boiler?"

"Don't know!"

Grabbing onto anything that floated, the crew and passengers gulped air.

Debris blanketed the muddy Mississippi. Floating timber, pieces of clothing, blue checked fabric. A minnow bucket bobbed on the churning waters.

Struggling to sit up, Amelia expected to see Austin Brown sweeping down upon them any minute. Her eyes widened when she saw a piece of wood bearing the name *Black Widow* float by. Her face broke into a weary smile. Not only had the *Mississippi Lady* blown up, but Austin's boat had met the same fate.

Pandemonium broke out as the crew of the *Mississippi Lady* whooped and hollered!

"We made it!"

"Praise the Lord!"

Holding on to Morgan, Amelia watched the last pieces of Brown's boat slowly sink into the Mississippi. She held her breath, waiting for bodies to surface. Releasing the breath slowly, she realized there would be none.

It was over. The adventure was finally over.

Amelia broke from Morgan's embrace and paddled to assist Pilar, who clung to Mahalia's neck as if it were a life raft. Niles had her by the shirt collar, helping to keep the young woman afloat.

Morgan checked on Izzy and Henry, who had little more than a few cuts and abrasions from the accident. Henry refused to complain. "At my age, I'm glad to still be here."

Izzy appeared not to have suffered anything other than a severe bout of indignity. The explosion had blown her false teeth out, and some fish was now likely proudly displaying the newfound choppers below the water — leastways that's what Niles said. The four spit water.

Niles said, "Are we going to swim for the bank?"

Morgan measured the distance. "The river is wide here. The younger ones can make it, but the older ones shouldn't try. I say we tread water for a bit. This is a heavily traveled channel; another boat will happen along shortly." He glanced at Izzy. "Can you make it until then?"

Izzy shook her head, refusing to speak.

"She can make it," Henry offered. "She don't talk with her teeth out."

Niles jerked his head in Amelia's direction, whose head was bobbing in the water. "Now that this is over, what are you going to do about her?"

Morgan traced the man's gaze. "What do you mean, 'do about her'? She's fine. She doesn't appear to have suffered any wounds."

"I can see she's *fine.* Mighty fine."

Izzy leaned over and pointed her finger sternly at him. "Time's a-wastin', young man."

The adventure was nearly over. Soon they would be on dry land, and the long-delayed trip to Mercy Flats could begin.

Elizabeth, who had apparently caught part of the conversation, paddled over to join the group. "Yeah, Kane. What are you going to do about her?"

Morgan shrugged. "I wasn't aware that my interest in Miss McDougal was that obvious."

"You're not going to let her get away, are you?" Elizabeth treaded water. "Let her walk out of your life as quickly as she entered, like a bull in a china closet?"

"I haven't thought much about the matter the past few hours." Gazes focused on the young woman who had literally turned Morgan Kane's life upside down.

Morgan cleared his throat. "I haven't decided what to do about Amelia McDougal."

Izzy frowned. "Well, you'd better be making up your mind, young'un. A woman ain't likely to wait forever for her man to come to his senses." Her gaze turned stern. "Heed my warning."

TWELVE

Two weeks later a sizable entourage of wagons topped the rise overlooking San Miguel mission in Mercy Flats, Texas.

The convent was there, just as Amelia had remembered. Broken hinges, a few scattered chickens, and tangled vines never looked so good. She drew a deep breath and looked at Morgan. "I'm home."

"That you are." He set the brake and permitted the women their first glance of their new home. Towering oaks sheltered the old mansion. Smoke curled from the stovepipe, no doubt a leftover from dinner.

Sighing, she glanced over her shoulder and smiled. "We're all home."

The women smiled, each making a comment about their new home.

"Beautiful."

"It looks so peaceful."

"It will be a joy to live here."

Of course, Abigail, Anne-Marie, and the

nuns would be delighted to see her and the newcomers she was bringing. The convent was the perfect ending to a less-than-perfect journey. Amelia's eyes scanned the grounds for sign of her sisters. The courtyard was empty. The sisters would be in early afternoon chapel. Amelia's pulse quickened. No use to get upset. Yet. Perhaps Abigail and Anne-Marie were inside, or perhaps they had taken a walk. Time passed slowly inside the building with the red clay roof.

If nothing else, Amelia's adventure had proven one thing to her. She had lost her taste for reckless escapades. She'd prefer to live a nice, sane life from now on, one devoid of excitement — especially constant turmoil. A passing ship had discovered the *Mississippi Lady*'s occupants floating in the water early morning. The violent thunderstorm had passed, and the dazed passengers drifted, waiting for help. They hadn't been in the water more than an hour before a small freighter happened along. The soggy group grabbed supportive hands and were helped aboard, where the survivors were fed a hot meal and plenty of black coffee. Even Izzy commented that it was the best coffee she'd ever tasted!

Amelia was confident that once she explained how she felt about Morgan to Abigail and Anne-Marie, they'd agree it was time for the McDougal sisters to change their ways. Since the talk with Morgan about integrity, she knew his was the life she wanted. She vowed to keep her new-found honor now that she was back.

Abigail and Anne-Marie may have wanted nothing to do with men, but they hadn't met Amelia's man yet.

"I still can't believe we're safe and have a new home. The Lord is surely good." Ria sighed.

Amelia reached for Mahalia's hand. "You, along with the others, can keep the mission going for many, many years." Her earlier conversation with Elizabeth and Morgan flashed though her mind. She was pretty sure that Morgan's earlier explanation of his and Elizabeth's strange relationship meant that he felt more than obligation to her. She prayed it was so. She felt sure he would offer to stay around for a while — perhaps delay his trip to Washington a week or so. A lot could happen in a week. A lot of good things. Amelia would love to stay here with the sisters and her newfound family, yet she had grown to appreciate an apple every now and then.

"You're the one I will miss most," Amelia had told Elizabeth the night before they left

New Orleans. "No one can be as ornery as you, and I'll have no one to have a meaningful argument with. Please say you'll come with us."

"There are too many now," Elizabeth had maintained.

"One more won't hurt." Taking Elizabeth by the shoulders, Amelia had made her face her. "Where will you go? The war's over, and you have no one. You said so yourself."

"I don't need anyone."

Amelia's eyes narrowed. "Everyone needs someone. That's just the way God made life work. Having friends is priceless, and you have ten now. How's that for good fortune?"

"There you go, being bossy again." Elizabeth tried to look perturbed, but Amelia knew she wasn't. Elizabeth wanted to go to Mercy Flats as much as the others, but Amelia could see that she felt she didn't have the right to intrude.

"You listen to me." Amelia squared Elizabeth's shoulders. "Someone's got to keep those ornery nuns and me under control, and name me one other person who is better equipped than you."

"Ornery sisters?"

"Believe me, the order can be a real handful when they take a notion."

And so all eyes focused on the convent, a

new start in life. It wasn't much, the Mission San Miguel — a few adobe buildings under the blazing sun — but it looked like bacon and Washington apples to Amelia.

The big hurdles were behind, with the exception of one.

Turning to Morgan, she asked quietly, "May I have a word with you in private, please?"

Removing his hat, Morgan wiped his forehead with his shirt sleeve before settling it back on his head.

He nodded and climbed down from the buckboard to follow her to a small clearing a short distance from the other wagons.

Locking her hands to her waist, Amelia began to pace, not sure where to begin. She had given her subject significant thought during the journey from New Orleans. In fact, it was all she had thought about during the long trip. She was aware Morgan was a man who would prefer conformity in a woman, but she was what she was. If she were meek, she would lose him, and she did not intend to lose him. Goodness knew she'd fought long and hard for his attention.

"Morgan," she began.

"Yes."

"I want you to know that I plan to purchase books on Washington Territory and read every last one of them, even if it takes me years." She wasn't much on reading, but that would change. She clasped her hands together tightly as her pacing picked up tempo.

"Go on."

"Yes, many books," she murmured. "All on Washington Territory, and I swear I'll study them carefully."

"You planning on visiting Washington?" His tone was casual, but she was encouraged to continue by the hint of interest she detected.

"Well, it's possible. I don't know if you've noticed, but I've been eating a lot of apples lately."

"Yes, that has come to my attention. Bacon is good, but not for every meal."

Her expression fell. "I love bacon." She brightened. "But I'm learning to like apples."

"I noticed you seem to lean toward the tarter ones lately. Jonathans, I believe?"

"Yes. Jonathans are my personal favorite."

His eyes twinkled "They're better for you than bacon."

"Yes. I've been thinking about coming to Washington," she mused. "If you want me to."

The moment of silence frightened her, but she was willing to wait for his consideration. After all, this was rather quick.

Removing his hat, he dusted it on the knees of his denims. "If I want you to," he repeated. "I don't recall the subject has ever come up."

She paused, turning to look at him. "I'm aware that Elizabeth, even though you both say you're not attracted to each other, would make a better wife."

Surprise flickered briefly across his features.

"But I could love you more. Now, I've been thinking. You have to return to Washington to run the orchards for Silas and Laura, and as big as they are, you really do need my help. Or someone's help." She retreated a step and met his steady gaze. "Wouldn't you agree?" She plunged on, afraid to face the risk of letting him answer. "I mean, four hands are better than two, besides which, if you're ever going to have children, you should start soon, or you'll be too old to enjoy them. Agreed?"

He nodded. "Agreed."

"And as far as I can tell, you don't have anyone in particular at this point that you want to marry. Am I right?"

"I wouldn't say 'no one,' but yes, I'm still single."

"So why don't we do this?" She started to pace again. "My sisters and I had made a blood pact to always stay together, but I can get out of it."

"You can get out of a blood pact?"

"Sure! When I tell them about you and how you saved my life and how badly you need a good, dependable, strong wife" — she emphasized the word *strong* — "to help pick apples, they'll understand."

"You're sure about that?"

She nodded solemnly. "I'm positive. They're very understanding people."

Running his hand through his hair, he glanced at the wagons.

"After we get the others settled, I'll have a nice little chat with my sisters, providing they're back —"

Tears sprang to her eyes. She was a bag of emotions now that the end of the long journey was finally in sight. If Abigail and Anne-Marie had not survived, she wasn't sure she could face a life without them. And if Morgan refused her, life would go on, but the joy within her would never be the same.

"The other women know my . . . feelings for you, so we can leave for Washington right away. I know you've been delayed longer than you planned," she conceded. "We can be on our way shortly." She met his steady gaze. "Agreed?"

True, it was a backdoor marriage proposal if there ever was one, and she knew he should be the one asking her. But she wasn't inclined to tradition. And asking him to marry her flat out seemed too pushy, even for a McDougal.

"Agreed?" she prompted when he just stood there looking at her. Great balls of fire! He had to agree. Now that he'd turned her life upside down, he couldn't walk away and pretend they'd never met. Pretend they'd never shared the past few weeks. Stolen kisses. Shared looks across the supper table that made a girl's heart tie into knots. What kind of man could do that? Not this man. Not her captain.

Turning away, Morgan appeared to be considering the idea. She worried her lower lip, waiting. This would have gone so much better if the roles were reversed. She didn't know much about this sort of thing, but she knew enough to wish that he'd taken the initiative. If he felt as strongly about her as she did him, he'd be doing the asking. The awful thought hit her. That was the problem. He didn't share her love — not the deep-down ache in the pit of his stomach that told him that his life would never be the same if he let her walk away.

When he turned back, he did so with a straight face. "I want to be sure I understand what you're saying. You are proposing marriage . . . to me?"

She nodded. "Yes, but only because I know you would never ask me."

"And how do you know that?"

"Well . . ." She thought for a moment. "We've only known each other a short while."

"That's for certain."

"And we've had very little time alone," she reasoned. Heat touched her cheeks, and she corrected herself. "Well, very little time together. So you really couldn't have fallen in love with me. I'm impetuous, so my falling in love with you isn't out of the ordinary. We both know I tend to be rather impulsive at times, but I always know what I want. At least, almost always, and in this instance, I know for certain that I want you."

He conceded the point. "Yes, you're all those — but a lot more, Amelia."

More? Her mind raced to find another one of her less-than-appealing ways. "I have been a considerable burden to you," she admitted, "so I understand why you wouldn't have thought of marriage this soon. I mean, marriage between you and me. But I can simplify things because I know how I am when everything is normal, and I know that if I set my mind to it, I could make you a fine wife. Maybe not as good as Elizabeth or someone like her, because, well, Elizabeth has been married before, and . . . well, you know . . ."

"I'm afraid I don't. Tell me."

"Well." This was embarrassing, but if they were going to be married, she supposed they'd have to get around to the subject sooner or later. "Elizabeth knows what's expected in marriage. I don't."

"You're talking about a man and wife's relationship after the vows are said."

She sighed. "I'm rattling on now. I am a bit nervous."

"What about . . . the intimacy?"

"Intimacy. Yes, that's the word I'm searching for. I'm not a baby. I know what marriage means, and I am more than willing to share my . . . home and my heart with you, if you agree.

"Now mind you, I've never done anything even remotely close to . . . that."

"I admire your frankness about a subject most women would never mention. It sounds as though you've given this matter considerable thought between the times

we've been outrunning Comanche, privateers, and exploding boilers. Frankly, I
haven't focused on much else."

She detected a teasing tone — but a sweet
one, in his voice. "Not considerable . . . but
enough to know what I want." She glanced
at him uneasily. "You don't mind, do you? I
mean, my thinking things like that about
you?"

"No," he offered graciously. "I don't
mind."

"Well," she continued. "What about me?
Are you looking forward to, you know, being married?"

His eyes skimmed her lazily. "I am."

"Oh." She smiled, loving him even more
for his understanding. "Then you're accept-
ing my proposal?" The air went out of her
with relief. She'd dreaded this moment
since she'd decided to propose to him,
which had been two days earlier.

"Morgan." Her voice suddenly sounded
small and uncertain. "What if something
bad has happened to Abigail and Anne-
Marie?" Amelia hadn't let herself dwell on
that possibility, but she must face the possibility now.

He reached out to take her hand. "Whatever awaits you here at the mission, I'll be
with you."

Lifting her eyes, she looked at him. "I'm scared," she whispered.

"I am too," he said softly. He took her hand and held it. They gazed at each other, and the same love that was in her eyes mirrored back from his.

"Does this mean that you accept my proposal and you'll come back?" She was afraid to hope or believe that he could ever be hers.

"No," he replied. "However, I have had the same thoughts you've expressed, and I've come to the conclusion that you would do me a great honor if you would accept mine."

Her eyes filled with joy. "You're proposing? To me?" Her voice dropped to a mere whisper. "You're actually asking me to marry you?"

"Yes, Amelia. I'm asking. I feel I've cheated you out of a decent courting period, but I'll make up for it." He winked. "You have my word."

"Oh. Well. Yes. Yes! A thousand times, yes!" She threw her arms around his neck ecstatically. Her gaze locked with his. "It isn't the amount of time that we've known each other that matters; it's the knowledge, the deep-down belief that we truly belong together, that counts."

"I agree. Completely." He drew her close for a long kiss.

Applause sounded from the wagons, and they broke apart, her gaze reluctant to leave his.

"Shall we go meet your soon-to-be new sisters-in-law?" she asked.

He extended his arm. "It would be my pleasure, Miss McDougal."

Arm in arm they walked back to the awaiting wagon. The future didn't frighten her so much anymore. With Morgan by her side, she could face anything. Even the loss of her beloved sisters.

If you've read Lori Copeland's first book in this series, *Sisters of Mercy Flats,* you may be wondering,
What happened with Abigail and Captain Barrett Drake?

And if you've read the second book, *My Heart Stood Still,* you may ask,
What about Anne-Marie and Creed Walker?

If that's you, read on and find out . . .

"You might as well come away from the window." Abigail watched as Anne-Marie lifted the mission parlor curtain again to peer out. If she'd looked out once, she'd looked out a hundred times this morning. "Creed will be back."

Her sister let the curtain drop back into place dispiritedly. "I wish I believed that as much as you do."

"He'll be back, just as Amelia will be here any day now." Abigail stitched the hem of a new shirt she was making for baby Daniel. She had to guess at the little boy's size. He had probably grown a mile since she'd left him last month. Only this morning a letter had arrived from the Mother Superior telling her how well he was doing. She had written that Daniel was growing like ragweed and was looking forward to the arrival of his new parents.

Resting the shirt on her lap, Abigail thought about Daniel's handsome, strong father, her new husband, Barrett Drake.

At first she had been worried that her sisters had met with ill fate, but barely a week after her arrival back at the mission, Anne-Marie returned. Now only Amelia remained absent. But Amelia was late for everything, so there was no real cause for alarm. She'd be back as surely as Anne-

Marie returned safely.

Leaning against the windowsill, Anne-Marie murmured, "I wonder what Creed is thinking these days? Do you think he will really come back for me?" Creed had been promised to another woman when he rescued Anne-Marie from the jail wagon, but by the end of their journey, both Anne-Marie and Creed Walker had fallen in love.

"Were you surprised when he asked you to marry him?" Abigail bit the thread in two and laid the needle aside.

"Very surprised, and thankful. I assumed he would honor his pledge to Berry Woman."

"But he didn't." Abigail smiled.

Abigail had married her rescuer, Barrett Drake, shortly after Anne-Marie's return. A smile crossed Abigail's lips when she thought about Barrett. She had thought she was grabbed by a twit of a shoe salesman, Mr. Hershall Digman. She stole his horse and rode off to the nearest town, not giving him another thought . . . until she discovered those secret papers in his saddlebags. Mr. Digman — Barrett Drake — turned out to be a Confederate spy, and it seemed the mismatched couple needed one another.

Anne-Marie's champion was a Crow warrior, Creed Walker. The relationship was loathing at first sight, but with bandits on their tail and a cache of gold to hide, Creed and Anne-Marie needed each other. Apparently for a lifetime. Barrett rode off a few days earlier to finalize his discharge from the service, but he would be home soon. This time, forever. Abigail and Creed had yet to exchange vows.

"Oh, Abigail. I long for Creed's return."

"He'll be back as soon as he ties up old business."

Turning away from the window, Anne-Marie flicked an imaginary piece of dust from a porcelain figure sitting on the table in front of the window. "Maybe. Remember how you used to tell us that men — all men — were no good?"

"Yes, but I was wrong."

"You sure were. So very wrong." Her sister playfully tapped the back of Abigail's head. "I am so very glad you were mistaken." She sobered. "What if Creed doesn't come back?"

"Don't be silly. He's madly in love with you." Abigail's eyes softened. "It's written all over the man's face."

Anne-Marie slowly stretched. "I don't understand what's keeping Amelia. She should be here by now." Neither sister thought otherwise. The McDougals were survivors. They would be reunited, but it was strange that Amelia was taking so long.

"How do you think she'll take the news of our marriages?" Anne-Marie said. "Especially since you've contended that men were horrible."

Abigail bit off a thread. "One look at Barrett and Creed and she'll understand."

"There is that pact we made." Anne-Marie had gravitated to the window again, and Abigail joined her there.

"You know," Abigail murmured in awe, "I would have never in a hundred years thought I would meet a man that I would fall so desperately in love with."

A sad smile touched the corners of Anne-Marie's mouth. "I know. And I still shudder when I think of how close I came to surrendering Creed to another woman."

Wrapping her arms around her sister's waist, Abigail hugged her. "We have very good men. Honorable, kind. We are blessed."

"Very — only what if something dreadful happened to Amelia?"

"We can't allow ourselves to consider the possibility. She's smart and practical . . . sometimes, even though she doesn't show it. She'll find a way home."

Abigail lifted the curtain to peer out when

a ruckus outside caught her attention. "What in heaven's name is going on?" Four buckboards had pulled into the courtyard, stirring up the guineas, that were making a terrible racket.

"Amelia! She's home!" Grinning, Abigail dropped the curtain back in place and gave Anne-Marie another hug. "See — I told you she'd be back!"

Running out to the courtyard, Abigail and Anne-Marie greeted Amelia with a round of long hugs and exuberant kisses.

"What took you so long?" Abigail exclaimed. "We were about to come looking for you!"

"You'll never believe what's happened," Amelia said breathlessly. "You see, this man, Morgan Kane, rescued me, and we rode to Galveston, and he gave me some money to buy passage on the ship back to Mercy Flats, but I foolishly decided that I wasn't going to do what he wanted me to do, so I went shopping, and before I knew it I had shopped too long to buy my passage on the ship back to Mercy Flats. I wandered around Galveston until I bumped into this man who I thought was a wonderful, generous person, but it turned out he was nothing but a scurrilous, evil man, and before I knew it I was abducted and thrown on a ship named the *Black Widow,* and this horrible man who I thought was a friend, named Austin Brown, was going to sell me to a scurrilous privateer, Dov Lanigan, but then this wonderful man, Morgan Kane, rescued me a second time from Brown and put me and my new friends on this old riverboat called the *Mississippi Lady,* whose crew were all as old as Sister Agnes!"

Abigail's eyes rounded. "No!"

"*Yes.* And then we were heading for New Orleans, where Captain Jean Louis and Morgan thought they could get me and the other women to safety, but then the engine broke down. Then, lo and behold, a few miles from New Orleans, a huge storm came up, and I was thrown overboard, and I thought I could hear Morgan calling for me to take his hand, but it wasn't Morgan. It was that scurrilous Brown in pursuit. He pulled me aboard his ship, but then Morgan took aim and let him have it with a Sharps rifle, and then all at once everyone was shooting at each other, and Captain Jean Louis said he'd have to make a run for it, which we did, but then the boilers on the *Mississippi Lady* overheated because we were throwing everything from bacon slices to kitchen benches in it, and all of a sudden there was this horrendous explosion, and I

310

was thrown out into the water again. Everyone started calling out their names, and I started crying because I was so happy no one was hurt, but then we still knew Austin Brown was after us. About that time, we noticed a piece of wood floating by that didn't belong to our boat, and we knew that Austin's boiler had blown too, so everyone was rejoicing that the chase was over, not that we were happy that folks died, but actually we were, since everybody aboard Austin Brown's boat was evil. Not one survived the blast."

She took a deep breath. "It took us a few days to arrange for wagons because I've brought all my marvelous new friends here because I wanted to and they had nowhere else to go." She took another deep breath. "I've invited the women to live here at the mission, and I had to convince them that the mission really needed them, but because most of the women didn't have anyplace to go, they decided they might as well come back with me. Their names are Pilar, Auria, Belicia, Ria, Mira, Bunny, Mahalia, Hester, Faith, and last but certainly not least, Elizabeth." Amelia reached out to take Elizabeth's hand. "She's my best friend." She took a third deep breath. "That's why I'm late."

The scary thing about the McDougal sisters was that they understood what the other ones were saying. Always.

Turning to Anne-Marie, Abigail grinned. "Didn't I tell you something simple like that had delayed her?"

The nuns came out to investigate the noise, and the reunion was complete. The mission grounds were filled with sounds of laughter and happiness as introductions were made all around.

Sister Lucille took the new ones under her wing and saw to their immediate comforts.

That evening everyone retired to rooms earlier than usual. The McDougal sisters were finally back in their own room, the one they'd shared since childhood. It was the first moment of privacy they'd shared.

Pulling a brush through her hair, Amelia stared at her reflection in the mirror. She had changed during a scant few weeks. Not only on the outside, but on the inside as well. She looked older. Wiser.

She blushed, recalling the embarrassing way she had proposed to Morgan earlier. He denied her request but spoke his desire. A smile touched her lips. He proposed — and that's really how marriage should be.

The man asking the woman. He truly was in love with her.

Lifting her finger, she touched her lips, his scent still lingering there. There had been barely time earlier for a brief stolen kiss in the dark foyer before retiring. She had yet to tell Abigail and Anne-Marie about him and the future they planned together. In all the excitement, he had been briefly introduced as the man who had been her rescuer.

"Abby," she mused thoughtfully. "Do you know anything about integrity?"

"Integrity?" Abigail thought for a moment. "It's something like honor?"

"Yes, something like that."

"I know a lot more than I did. Barrett has shown me the meaning of keeping one's word. He has taught me right from wrong. I am so ashamed of what we have done, Amelia."

Amelia nodded. "So am I. What about you, Anne-Marie? Do you know anything about integrity?"

"I know honor and integrity are good things among men. Creed is the most honorable man I have ever known. And I thank God for the day he rescued me from that jail wagon."

"Integrity and honor are good." Laying

her brush aside, Amelia turned to face her sisters. "From now on, I intend to be filled with character and truthfulness."

Gathering around her feet, her sisters nodded in agreement. "Me too," Abigail admitted. "Our old ways are over."

"I've given the matter considerable thought, and I agree," Anne-Marie said softly. "If we ask the Lord for forgiveness, and if we truly change our ways, He will grant it. We'll work, plant a second garden, take in sewing, and even wash to earn money for the mission."

Joining hands, the women prayed together for grace and forgiveness for their past ways.

"You know this means we can no longer do what we did," Anne-Marie said when the confessions ended.

"That's fine with me," both Amelia and Abigail voiced.

Amelia explained how the women she'd brought with her were truly gifted and how they would stay on and run the mission for the aging nuns when the time came for the McDougal sisters to leave. The mission would be in good hands. The good sisters could rest assured of that.

The women fell silent.

"You know, there is the other matter of authorities," Anne-Marie said quietly. "We are still wanted by the state for our crimes. God will forgive us, but Texas won't."

"We must turn ourselves in," Abigail said.

"No!" Amelia couldn't turn herself in to the authorities! Not now that God had led her to Morgan and now that the love of her life returned her feelings. But her sin, though forgiven, would hold consequences.

Honor and integrity — each sister wanted those attributes. But their former lives hung around their necks like millstones.

"I have a good deal of gold," Anne-Marie said. "Perhaps we could repay those we have wronged."

Abigail frowned. "Where did you get a great deal of gold?"

"It's a long story best saved for another day. But I have all the money we, or the convent, will ever need."

"How would we ever be able to find everyone we've wronged?" Amelia shook her head. "It wouldn't be possible."

"Actually," Anne-Marie mused, "the McDougal sisters, as we knew them, died that day in the jail wagon accident."

The thought was so grave, the sisters paused to ponder the somber notion.

Reaching for the hands of her sisters, Anne-Marie said softly, "I can't exactly explain what's happened to each of us since the day the Comanche attacked the wagon, but we've changed. Our hearts have changed."

Each sister marveled at the differences they witnessed in each other. They seemed older now, mature and compassionate. Undoubtedly the authorities assumed that they'd been carried off by the Comanche and either killed or taken as brides. The empty jail wagon and the driver with an arrow through his heart would have sealed that conviction.

"I know what happened to me," Amelia whispered. "I fell in love. With God, with goodness and purity, and with Morgan."

No one spoke for a moment. The magnitude of the thought hung in the air.

"With a man," Amelia clarified. She waited for the repelling looks that would surely be coming.

"With Morgan Kane," Anne-Marie supplied.

Abigail glanced at Anne-Marie, and the sisters broke into grins.

"Aren't you mad at me?" Amelia slid to her knees to face them. "I mean, there is the blood pact and all. But I love Morgan . . . no, I *adore* this man, and I asked him to marry me this morning."

"Amelia!" Anne-Marie scolded. "You

316

asked him?"

"Yes, but he asked me back."

"Silly goose!" Abigail hugged her.

"Then you're not mad?" Amelia asked, hardly daring to believe they were taking the betrayal so well.

"We're not mad." Grinning, Abigail held out her left hand, flashing the plain gold band on her third finger. "I married my rescuer, Barrett Drake, two days ago. He's the most wonderful man in the whole wide world."

Shrieks of joy broke out as Amelia and Abigail hugged one another. "I can't believe it!"

"I can't either."

"A man! We each fell in love with a *man*!"

"But what men!"

Anne-Marie shared their excitement with a beaming smile. "I, too, fell in love with my rescuer, Creed Walker."

"No!" Amelia hugged her sister tighter. Who could have imagined all three McDougals would find true love in such unlikely circumstances?

The excitement faded, and the girls shared their adventures of the past weeks. Amelia regaled the women with tales from aboard the *Mississippi Lady* with Morgan and the women who accompanied her. Izzy, Niles,

Ryder, Henry, and Captain Jean Louis came next. She vowed that her adventures were the most exciting times she'd ever experienced, but she didn't care to ever relive them.

Abigail spoke of how Barrett Drake had rescued her from the jail wagon, the flight from the Comanche, and the trials and tribulations they had endured on the return trip to the mission. She spoke of a marriage proposal from a man named Doyle Dobbs and, of course, baby Daniel, the orphaned infant whom Abigale and Barrett now parented. It seems Anne-Marie and Amelia had acquired a nephew during their difficulties.

"Creed Walker rescued me," said Anne-Marie. "He, along with John Quincy Adams, brought me to safety. Storm Rider, Creed's Indian name, and Storm Rider's blood brother, Bold Eagle, and his people took me in and gave me shelter." Her voice softened when she told of Berry Woman, the young maiden Creed was pledged to marry but who had been mauled by a bear and lay gravely wounded for weeks.

"You, Creed, and Quincy *tricked a crooked banker,* Loyal Streeter, out of a huge gold shipment?" Amelia exclaimed.

Anne-Marie nodded. "We did, and though

the deed was warranted, my life of playing Robin Hood is over. I will never take from another what isn't mine."

"Amen," Amelia added.

"The same goes here." Abigail reached out, and the girls made their usual solemn pact sign. Fists on top of each other, stacked high. Abigail's fist sealed the promise. Reaching over, she slipped her arm around Anne-Marie and held her for a moment. "We are all greatly blessed," she whispered.

Amelia joined in, hugging Anne-Marie too. Tears welled in her eyes. She was home. Finally home. "Where are these two wonderful men, Barrett and Creed?" The tall savage who had ridden off with her sister had indeed been an incredibly handsome figure.

Abigail's eyes filled with love. "Barrett has gone to finalize his papers with the government; Creed" — she glanced at Anne-Marie — "is gone, but he will return soon." She changed subjects. "I hate to ask, but do you think that Ryder or Henry could go look for the cow in the morning? The animal ran away during a storm, and the sisters can't find her."

Amelia's face fell. "Oh. Sister Agnes has to go without cream in her coffee?" The good sister laced her morning cup heavily with the rich butterfat.

"Yes, and I promise you'll hear about it rather quickly."

"I'll ask 'Enry first thing in the morning." Amelia giggled and then explained how she'd misunderstood the man's name for a day or two.

"His teeth are pretty big, aren't they?"

Amelia nodded. "Gigantic — but you won't notice after a while because he's so good and kind. Izzy says it's a man's heart that counts."

The girls talked long into the night, trying to analyze their new feelings toward men.

"Barrett had been hesitant about remarrying," Abigail admitted. "But in the end, he realized we were meant for each other."

"I can hardly wait to meet Daniel." Amelia shifted. "And Barrett, of course. I know I will love them both. Morgan and I haven't set a date for our marriage yet because we haven't had time to catch our breaths, but I want it to be soon — very soon." She went on to explain about Silas and Laura and how her man needed to be in the apple orchards in Washington as quickly as possible.

Anne-Marie cocked a brow. "You detest apples."

Amelia hugged a feather pillow to her

chest. "Not anymore."

"Barrett and I will be leaving to pick up Daniel soon and then head on to Louisiana," Abigail said. "I will miss you both dreadfully, and the good sisters, but we will write often."

"I will pray for each of you a world of happiness," Anne-Marie said. "Both Barrett and Morgan sound like wonderful choices. Creed has asked the good sisters for my hand in marriage, but everything is happening so fast, we haven't had time to set a date either." She paused. "Perhaps he has changed his mind. He was betrothed to another when we first met."

Amelia frowned. "He is?"

"Was," Anne-Marie corrected. "We got word shortly before we rode into the mission that the woman married another man."

"But wasn't she pledged to marry this Creed?"

Anne-Marie smiled. "It's complicated. Just say that Creed and I know our futures are with each other. We've made sound choices."

"We didn't make the choice. God did," Amelia confessed. Scooting closer, she reached for Anne-Marie's hand. "I can't wait to meet this Creed Walker."

A smile escaped her sister. "He's all mine.

Hands off."

"Oh, I'm perfectly happy with the man God gave me." Amelia's stomach churned at the notion of being separated from Anne-Marie and Abigail, but love often called for great sacrifice — that much she had learned.

And learning, for the McDougal sisters, was progress.

EPILOGUE

There couldn't have been a prettier sight than the sun resting over the newly leaved treetops in a fiery ball when Morgan Kane and Amelia McDougal exchanged vows on the twenty-first day of May.

The end of a beautiful day, one like no other, befitted this sacred moment.

From Pilar all the way to Elizabeth, these special women were dressed in pretty calico that Faith and Hester had sewn for the occasion.

Abigail and Anne-Marie stood beside Amelia, beaming. Like all things in their sister's life, her wedding was unconventional. Father Luis, very doddering now, performed the ceremony, his voice faltering at times when he forgot where he was.

Amelia had chosen to marry Morgan Kane as dawn broke, in the main convent hall, where morning vespers took place. Today was far from an ending. Today was a new beginning. The tolling bell in the steeple rang out pure joy on this flowering daffodil, late spring morning.

Morgan stole Amelia's breath away today. He stood tall, durable, and handsome in a black linen suit. The sun shot glints of gold in his dark hair, and his eyes danced with a twinkle that couldn't be mistaken for anything but love.

Barrett Drake stood beside his bride, Abigail, and her cheeks still flushed in his presence.

"Do you, Morgan Franklin Kane, take this woman, Amelia . . ."

Amelia was aware that Anne-Marie stood close, her eyes closed, silently repeating the vow to Creed Walker. Creed had been a busy man. Even today his tall form was missing in the crowd of well-wishers. So many loose ends to tie up after the war. Amelia could almost hear Anne-Marie's hushed whispers as she followed the ceremony. "I take thee, Creed Walker, as my wedded husband, to love, honor, and —"

"Obey," a deep voice interrupted softly in Anne-Marie's ear. "Hello, my darling."

Whirling, Anne-Marie met Creed's gaze staring somberly back at her. Wearing a pristine white shirt, a black frock coat and trousers, he looked magnificent.

"Creed!" she whispered. The couple dropped back from the wedding party, speaking in hushed tones. "I've been so worried about you! What's kept you so long?"

"Business matters took longer than expected, but I'm home for good." His eyes drank deeply of her, and her cheeks warmed with the loving perusal. Drawing her to him, Creed kissed her like a man who feared he might never again hold the woman he loved in his arms.

"I have missed you so deeply," she whispered against his lips.

"It's been an eternity since I held you."

Soft kisses prevented explanations. Neither was inclined to talk at the moment. The priest's words penetrated but barely. Creed was home. In her arms. Forever.

When their lips finally parted, Anne-Marie drew back ever so slightly until her eyes met his. "The army has released you from duty?"

"They have. Haven't you heard? The war is over."

"Yes, I heard. Praise God."

The applause as Amelia and Morgan finished their vows filled the background, and the groom swept his bride in his arms and kissed her. Anne-Marie's grip on Creed tightened. "You're really not heartbroken about losing Berry Woman to Plain Weasel?" she asked, praying, praying so desperately this moment that brought Amelia such joy would not bring Anne-Marie utter disillusionment.

"Disappointed? Me, disappointed?" It was Creed who grinned this time. "I was so disappointed that I gave Plain Weasel fifteen blankets and ten horses, and I threw in my saddle when I congratulated him."

"Oh, Creed!" She kissed him wildly, caring not that Sister Agnes and Sister Lucille looked on with their mouths agape.

Creed's arms encircled her possessively. "I love you, Anne-Marie, and I've missed you so much it hurt." He buried his face in her neck and held her tightly. "You're never going to be out of my sight again."

"I never doubted your word, not for a moment." Never deep in her heart had she truly doubted.

He met her gaze solidly. "Want to get married, Miss McDougal?"

"Yes, Mr. Walker. I surely do."

He offered his arm.

"Now? Right now?" She glanced at Amelia. She was the bride. This was her special day, not Anne-Marie's. She cupped his proud, handsome features in her hands and then pressed her lips to his to seal the words. "We have so much to catch up on. Abigail married her rescuer, Barrett Drake. Amelia just married her rescuer, Morgan Kane. Then I have to tell you about Amelia's adventures — you would not believe what happened to her. She was in a steamboat accident and survived! And Abigail — she thought she was rescued by this really strange shoe salesman, but he turned out to be working for the government, just like Amelia's new husband."

When she saw hurt enter his eyes, she rushed on. "Creed, I want to marry you so much, but we can't do this to Morgan and Amelia. It wouldn't be fair. This is their day — their very special day. But tomorrow — I will marry you tomorrow." Everyone would still be in a festive mood. She could borrow Amelia's dress, and enough food was prepared for the momentous occasion to feed an army.

Creed whispered against her lips. "I can't wait that long. I rode in late last night and happened to speak to Morgan Kane and Amelia."

She turned quizzical. "You saw them before you saw me?"

"I had a purpose, and I thought you would be asleep. It was well past midnight when I rode in."

"What could you possibly have to say to Morgan and Amelia? You don't know either of them."

"I met Amelia earlier, when I brought you home."

"I know — but briefly. Why would you want to see her and not me?"

"I had something I needed to ask."

"What?"

He sighed. "You're a persistent little gnat. Since so much happiness is gathered — the sisters, your sisters, and friends — I thought we might combine a wedding ceremony . . . or at least share one. Amelia squealed when I asked, so I took that to mean she agreed. She said our marriage would make the day that much more special. The only request was that she and Morgan exchange vows first. So she could taunt you about it." He flashed a silent apology. "I promised I would repeat her exact words."

Anne-Marie drew back. "Are you serious?" She glanced down at what she had thought was a bridesmaid gown when she dressed earlier. "But my dress . . ."

He gently tipped her face back to meet his. "Does a dress matter?"

Straightening, she met his gaze. "Not in the least — but if I'd only known, I would have dressed more appropriately."

He paused. "You're my bride, and I don't care what you're wearing. The only thing on my mind is you."

"Good enough." She gave him her sweetest smile. "Let's get married."

Slipping her arm through his, Anne-Marie led her man to Father Luis and the rest of the assembled wedding party. No one appeared to be too surprised by a second ceremony. By now Mercy Flats, Texas, was used to the McDougal sisters.

And the good Lord knew everyone would rest easier now that they'd gotten those three feisty gals settled.

ABOUT THE AUTHOR

Lori Copeland is the author of more than 100 titles, including *The Preacher's Lady* and *The Healer's Touch*. Her beloved novel *Stranded in Paradise* is now a Hallmark Channel Original Movie. Her stories have developed a loyal following among her rapidly growing fans in the inspirational market. She lives in the beautiful Ozarks with her husband, Lance.

The employees of Thorndike Press hope you have enjoyed this Large Print book. All our Thorndike, Wheeler, and Kennebec Large Print titles are designed for easy reading, and all our books are made to last. Other Thorndike Press Large Print books are available at your library, through selected bookstores, or directly from us.

For information about titles, please call:
  (800) 223-1244

or visit our Web site at:
  http://gale.cengage.com/thorndike

To share your comments, please write:
  Publisher
  Thorndike Press
  10 Water St., Suite 310
  Waterville, ME 04901